"Your father ***take a bride."***

Caroline winced. "I'm sorry. I understand you don't want me here, but for the children's sake, at least let me help for a day or two until you come up with another arrangement."

Wade rubbed the ache in his temple again, the weight of his responsibilities cumbersome and heavy.

What would be the harm in letting her help for a day or two?

Like it or not, she was connected to him now by virtue of their parents' hasty marriage. And this way he could at least keep an eye on her. If she and her father were cooking up some kind of scam together, then he might be wise to remember his brother's favorite saying. *Keep your friends close and your enemies closer.*

What better way to keep her close than by having her right here in his own home?

Dear Reader,

This beautiful month of April we have six very special reads for you, starting with *Falling for the Boss* by Elizabeth Harbison, this month's installment in our FAMILY BUSINESS continuity. Watch what happens when two star-crossed high school sweethearts get a second chance—only this time they're on opposite sides of the boardroom table! Next, bestselling author RaeAnne Thayne pays us a wonderful and emotional visit in Special Edition with her new miniseries, THE COWBOYS OF COLD CREEK. In *Light the Stars,* the first book in the series, a frazzled single father is shocked to hear that his mother (not to mention babysitter) eloped—with a supposed scam artist. So what is he to do when said scam artist's lovely daughter turns up on his doorstep? Find out (and don't miss next month's book in this series, *Dancing in the Moonlight).* In Patricia McLinn's *What Are Friends For?,* the first in her SEASONS IN A SMALL TOWN duet, a female police officer is reunited—with the guy who got away. Maybe she'll be able to detain him this time….

Jessica Bird concludes her MOOREHOUSE LEGACY series with *From the First,* in which Alex Moorehouse finally might get the woman he could never stop wanting. Only problem is, she's a recent widow—and her late husband was Alex's best friend. In Karen Sandler's *Her Baby's Hero,* a couple looks for that happy ending even though the second time they meet, she's six months' pregnant with his twins! And in *The Last Cowboy* by Crystal Green, a woman desperate for motherhood learns that "the last cowboy will make you a mother." But real cowboys don't exist anymore…or do they?

So enjoy, and don't forget to come back next month. Everything will be in bloom….

Have fun.

Gail Chasan
Senior Editor

LIGHT THE STARS

RAEANNE THAYNE

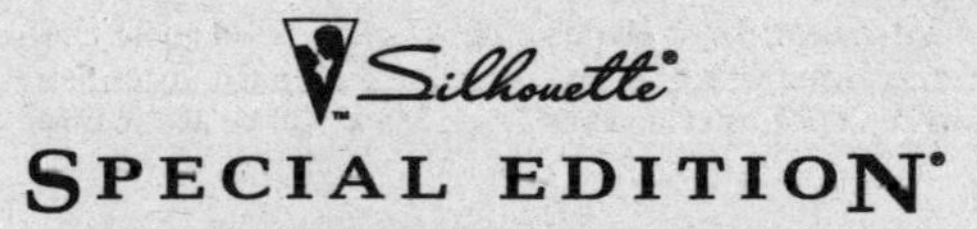

Published by Silhouette Books
America's Publisher of Contemporary Romance

ISBN 0-373-24748-6

LIGHT THE STARS

This edition published by arrangement with Harlequin Books S.A.

Visit Silhouette Books at www.eHarlequin.com

Printed in U.S.A.

Books by RaeAnne Thayne

Silhouette Special Edition

††*Light the Stars* #1748

Silhouette Intimate Moments

The Wrangler and the Runaway Mom #960
Saving Grace #995
Renegade Father #1062
**The Valentine Two-Step* #1133
**Taming Jesse James* #1139
**Cassidy Harte and the Comeback Kid* #1144
The Quiet Storm #1218
Freefall #1239
†*Nowhere To Hide* #1264
†*Nothing To Lose* #1321
†*Never Too Late* #1364
The Interpreter #1380

*Outlaw Hartes
†The Searchers
††The Cowboys of Cold Creek

RAEANNE THAYNE

finds inspiration in the beautiful northern Utah mountains where she lives with her husband and three children. Her books have won numerous honors, including a RITA® Award nomination and several *Romantic Times BOOKclub* reviewer's choice nominations. RaeAnne loves to hear from readers. She can be reached through her Web site at www.raeannethayne.com or at P.O. Box 6682 North Logan, UT 84341.

To Gail Chasan, for helping me reach my own dreams.
Many, many thanks.

Chapter One

On his thirty-sixth birthday, Wade Dalton's mother ran away.

She left him a German chocolate cake on the kitchen counter, two new paperback mysteries by a couple of his favorite authors and a short but succinct note in her loopy handwriting.

> Honey,
>
> Happy birthday. I'm sorry I couldn't be there to celebrate with you but by the time you read this we'll be in Reno and I'll be the new Mrs. Quinn Montgomery. I know you'll think I should have told you but my huggy bear thought it would be better this way. More romantic. Isn't that sweet? You'll love him, I promise! He's handsome, funny, and makes

me feel like I can touch my dreams again. Tell the children I love them and I'll see them soon.

P.S. Nat's book report is due today. Don't let her forget it!

P.P.S. Sorry to leave you in the lurch like this but I figured you, Seth and Nat could handle things without me for a week. Especially you. You can handle anything.

Don't take this wrong, son, but it doesn't hurt for you to remember your children are more important than your blasted cattle.

Be back after the honeymoon.

Wade stared at the note for a full five minutes, the only sound in the Cold Creek Ranch kitchen the ticking of the pig-shaped clock Andi had loved above the stove and the refrigerator compressor kicking to life.

What the hell was he supposed to do now?

His mother and this huggy bear creature couldn't have chosen a worse time to pull their little disappearing act. Marjorie knew it, too, blast her hide. He needed her help! He had six hundred head of cattle to get to market before the snow flew, a horse show and auction in Cheyenne in a few weeks, and a national TV news crew coming in less than a week to film a feature on the future of the American cattle ranch.

He was supposed to be showing off the groundbreaking innovations he'd made to the ranch in the last few years, showing the Cold Creek in the best possible light.

How was he supposed to make sure everything was ready and running smoothly while he changed Cody's diapers and chased after Tanner and packed Nat's lunch?

He read the note again, anger beginning to filter through the dismayed shock. Something about what she had written seemed to thrum through his consciousness like a distant, familiar guitar chord. He was trying to figure out what when he heard the back-porch door creak and a moment later his youngest brother stumbled into the kitchen, bleary-eyed and in need of a shave.

"Coffee. I need it hot and black and I just realized I'm out down at my place."

Wade glared at him, seizing on the most readily available target for his frustration and anger. "You look like hell."

Seth shrugged. "Got in late. It was ladies' night down at the Bandito and I couldn't leave all those sweet girls shooting pool by themselves. Where's the coffee?"

"There isn't any coffee. Or breakfast, either. I don't suppose you happened to see Mom sneaking out at two in the morning when you were dragging yourself and, no doubt, one or two of those sweet girls back to the guesthouse?"

His brother blinked a couple of times to clear the remaining cobwebs from his brain. "What?"

Wade tossed the note at him and Seth scrubbed his bleary eyes before picking it up. A range of emotions flickered across his entirely too charming features—shock and confusion, then an odd pensiveness that raised Wade's hackles.

"Did you know about this?" he asked.

Seth slumped into a kitchen chair, avoiding his gaze. "Not this, precisely."

"What *precisely* did you know about what our dear mother's been up to?" Wade bit out.

"I knew she was e-mailing some guy she met through that life coach she's been talking to. I didn't realize it was serious. At least not run-off-to-Reno serious."

Suddenly this whole fiasco made a grim kind of sense and Wade realized what about Marjorie's note had struck that odd, familiar chord. *By the time you read this I'll be the new Mrs. Quinn Montgomery,* she had written.

Montgomery was the surname of the crackpot his mother had shelled out a small fortune to in the last six months, all in some crazy effort to better her life.

Caroline Montgomery.

He knew the name well since he'd chewed Marjorie out plenty the last time he'd balanced her checkbook for her and had found the name written on several hefty checks.

This was all this Caroline Montgomery's fault. It had to be. She must have planted ideas in Marjorie's head about how she wasn't happy, about how she needed more out of life. Fun, excitement. Romance. Then she introduced some slick older man—a brother? An uncle?—to bring a little spice into a lonely widow's world.

What had been so wrong with Marjorie's life, anyway, that she'd needed to find some stranger to fix it?

Okay, his mother had a few odd quirks. Today was not only his birthday, it was exactly the eighteen-year anniversary of his father's death and in those years, his mother had pursued one wacky thing after another. She did yoga, she balanced her chakras instead of her checkbook, she sponsored inflammatory little book-club meetings at the Pine Gulch library where she and her cronies read every controversial feminist, male-bashing self-help book they could find.

He had tried to be understanding about it all. Marjorie's marriage to Hank Dalton hadn't exactly been a happy one. His father had treated his mother with the same cold condescension he'd wielded like a club against his children. Once his father's death had freed Marjorie from that oppressive influence, Wade couldn't blame her for taking things a little too far in the opposite direction.

Besides, when he'd needed her in those terrible, wrenching days after Andrea's death, Marjorie had come through. Without him even having to ask, she'd packed up her crystals and her yoga mat and had moved back to the ranch to help him with the kids. He would have been lost without her, a single dad with three kids under the age of six, one of them only a week old.

He knew she wasn't completely happy with her life but he'd never thought she would go this far. She wouldn't have, he thought, if it hadn't been for this scheming Caroline Montgomery and whatever male relative she was in cahoots with.

He heard a belligerent yell coming from upstairs and wanted to pound his head on the table a few times. Six-thirty in the morning and it was already starting. How the hell was he going to do this?

"Want me to get Cody?" Seth asked as the cries rose in volume. *Gramma, Gramma, Gramma.*

Wade had to admit, the offer was a tempting one, but he forced himself to refuse. They were *his* children and he was the one who would have to deal with them.

He took off his denim jacket and hung his Stetson on the hook by the door.

"I'm on it. Just go take care of the stock and then we've all got to bring in the last hay crop we cut yesterday. The weather report says rain by afternoon so we've got to get it in fast. I'll figure something out with the kids and get out there to help as soon as I can."

Seth opened his mouth to say something then must have thought better of it. He nodded. "Right. Good luck."

You're going to need it. His brother left the words unspoken but Wade heard them anyway.

He couldn't agree more.

Two hours later, Wade was rapidly coming to the grim realization that he was going to need a hell of a lot more than luck.

"Hold still," he ordered a squirmy, giggling Cody as he tried to stick on a diaper. Through the open doorway into the kitchen, he could hear Tanner and Natalie bickering.

"Daaaad," his eight-year-old daughter called out, "Tanner's flicking Cheerios at me. Make him stop! He's getting the new shirt Grandma bought me all wet and blotchy!"

"Tanner, cut it out," he hollered. "Nat, if you don't quit stalling over your breakfast, you're going to miss the bus and I don't have time to drive you today."

"You never have time for anything," he thought he heard her mutter but just then he felt an ominous warmth hit his chest. He looked down to the changing table to find Cody grinning up at him.

"Cody pee pee."

Wade ground his back teeth, looking down at the wet stain spreading across his shirt. "Yeah, kid, I kind of figured that out."

He quickly fastened the diaper and threw on the

overalls and Spider-Man shirt Cody insisted on wearing, all the while aware of a gnawing sense of inadequacy in his gut.

He wasn't any good at this. He loved his kids but it had been a whole lot easier being their father when Andrea was alive.

She'd been the one keeping their family together. The one who'd scheduled immunizations and fixed Nat's hair into cute little ponytails and played Chutes and Ladders for hours at a time. His role had been the benevolent dad who showed up at bedtime and sometimes broke away from ranch chores for Sunday brunch.

The two years since her death had only reinforced how inept he was at the whole parenting gig. If it hadn't been for Marjorie coming to his rescue, he didn't know what he would have done.

Probably flounder around cluelessly, just like he was doing now, he thought.

He started to carry Cody back to the kitchen to finish his breakfast but the toddler was having none of it. "Down, Daddy. Down," he ordered, bucking and wriggling worse than a calf on his way to an appointment with the castrator.

Wade set his feet on the ground and Cody raced toward the kitchen. "Nat, can you watch Cody for a minute?" he called. "I've got to go change my shirt."

"Can't," she hollered back. "The bus is here."

"Don't forget your book report," he remembered at the last minute, but the door slammed on his last word and he was pretty sure she hadn't heard him.

With a quick order to Tanner to please behave himself for five minutes, he carried Cody upstairs with him and grabbed his last clean shirt out of the closet. The least his mother could have done was wait until *after* laundry day to pull her disappearing act, he thought wryly. Now he was going to have to do that, too.

He grabbed Cody and headed back down the stairs. They had nearly reached the bottom when the doorbell pealed.

"I'll get it," Tanner yelled and headed for the front door, still in his pajamas.

"No, me! Me!" Not to be outdone, Cody squirmed out of Wade's arms and slid down the last few steps. Wade wasn't sure how they did it, but both boys beat him to the door, even though he'd been closer.

Tanner opened it, then turned shy at the strange woman standing before him. Wade couldn't blame him. Their visitor was lovely, he observed as he reached the door behind his sons, with warm, streaky brown hair pulled back into a smooth twisty thing, eyes the color of hot chocolate on a cold winter day and graceful, delicate features.

She wore a tailored russet jacket, tan slacks and a crisp white shirt, with a chunky bronze necklace and matching earrings, a charm bracelet on one arm and a slim gold watch on the other.

Wade had no idea who she was and she didn't seem in any hurry to introduce herself. Probably some tourist who'd taken the wrong road out of Jackson, he thought, and needed help finding her way.

Finally he spoke.

"Can I help you?"

"Oh. Yes." Color flared on those high cheekbones and she blinked a few times as if trying to compose herself. "The sign out front said the Cold Creek Ranch. Is this the right place?"

No. Not a lost tourist. As Tanner peeked around Wade's legs and Cody held his chubby little arms out to be lifted again, Wade's gaze traveled from the woman's pretty, streaky hair to her expensive leather shoes, looking for some clue as to what she might be doing on his front porch.

If she was some kind of ranch supply salesperson, she was definitely a step above the usual. He had a lowering suspicion he'd buy whatever she was selling.

"You found us."

Relief flickered across her expressive features. "Oh, I'm so glad. The directions weren't exactly clear and I stopped at two other ranches before this one. I'd like to see Marjorie Dalton, please."

Yeah, wouldn't they all like to see her right about now? "There I'm afraid you're out of luck. She's not here."

Right before his eyes, the lovely, self-assured woman on his porch seemed to fold into herself. Her shoulders sagged, her mouth drooped and she closed her eyes. When she opened them, he saw for the first time the weariness there and was uncomfortably aware of an odd urge to comfort her, to tuck her close and assure her everything would be all right.

"Can you tell me…that is, do you know where I might find her?"

He didn't want to spill his mother's whereabouts to some strange woman, no matter how she mysteriously plucked all his protective strings. "Why don't you tell me your business with her and I'll get her a message?"

"It's complicated. And personal."

"Then you'll have to come back in a week or so."

He had to hope by then Marjorie would come to her senses and be back where she belonged.

"A week?" His visitor blanched. "Oh no! I'm too late. She's not here, is she?"

"That's what I said, isn't it?"

"No, I mean she's really not here. She's not just in town shopping or something. They've run off, haven't they?"

He stared at her, wariness blooming in his gut. "Who are you and what do you want with my mother?"

The woman gave a weary sigh. "You must be Wade. I've heard a lot about you. My name is Caroline Montgomery. I've been in correspondence with Marjorie for the last six months. I don't know how to tell you this, Mr. Dalton, but I think Marjorie has run off with my father."

The big, gorgeous man standing in front of her with one cute little boy hanging off his belt loop and another in his arms didn't look at all shocked by her bombshell. No, shock definitely wasn't the emotion that hardened his mouth and tightened those stunning blue eyes into dime slots.

He brimmed with fury—toe-curling, hair-scorching anger. Caroline took an instinctive step back, until the weave of her jacket bumped against the peeled log of his porch.

"Your father!" he bit out. "I should have known. What is it they say about apples not falling far from the tree?"

Maybe if she wasn't so blasted tired from traveling all night, she might have known what he was talking about. "I'm sorry?"

"What's the matter, lady? You weren't bilking

Marjorie out of enough with your hefty life-coaching fees so you decided to go for the whole enchilada?"

She barely had time to draw a breath before he went on.

"Quite a racket you and your old man have. How many wealthy widows have you pulled this on? You drag them in, worm out all the details about their financial life, then your old man moves in for the kill."

Caroline wanted to sway from the force of the blow that hit entirely too close to home. She felt sick, hideously sick, and bitterly angry that Quinn would once more put her in this position. How else was all this supposed to look, especially given her father's shady past?

She wouldn't give this arrogant man the satisfaction of knowing he'd drawn blood, though. Instead she forced her spine to straighten, vertebra by vertebra.

"You're wrong."

"Am I?"

"Yes! I was completely shocked by this sudden romance. My father said nothing about it to me—I didn't know he and Marjorie had even met until he sent me an e-mail last night telling me he was flying out to meet her and they were heading straight from here to Reno."

"Why should I believe you?"

"I don't care if you believe me or not! It's the truth."

How much of her life had been spent defending herself because of something Quinn had done? She had vowed she was done with it but now she wondered grimly if she ever would be.

What was Quinn up to? Just once, she wished she knew. With all her heart, she wanted to believe his sudden romance was the love match he had intimated in his e-mail.

> I never meant for this to happen. It took us both completely by surprise. But in just a few short months I've discovered I can't live without her. Marjorie is my other half—the missing piece of my life's puzzle. She knows all my mistakes, all my blemishes, but she loves me anyway. How lucky am I?

Caroline was romantic enough to hope Quinn's hearts-and-flowers e-mail was genuine. Her mother had been dead for twenty-two years now and, as far as she knew, her father's love life was as exciting as her own—i.e., about as thrilling as watching paint dry.

But how could she trust his word, after years of his schemes and swindles? Especially when the missing piece of his life's puzzle was one of *her* clients? She couldn't. She just *couldn't.*

What if Quinn was spinning some new scam? Something involving Marjorie Dalton—and tangentially, Caroline's reputation? She would be ruined. Everything she had worked so hard for these last five years, her safe, comfortable, *respectable* life, would crumble away like a sugar castle in a hurricane.

Caroline knew what was at stake: her reputation, which in the competitive world of life coaching was everything. As soon as she'd read his e-mail, she had been struck with a familiar cold dread and knew she would have to track him down to gauge his motives for herself—or to talk him out of this crazy scheme to marry a woman he had only corresponded with via e-mail.

Her first self-help book was being released in five

months and if her publisher caught wind of this, they would not be happy. She'd be lucky if her book wasn't yanked right off the schedule.

That's why she had traveled all night to find herself here at nine in the morning, facing down a gorgeous rancher and his two cute little boys.

But she wasn't going to accomplish anything by antagonizing Marjorie's son, she realized. She took a deep, cleansing breath and forced her expression into a pleasant smile, her voice into the low, calming tones she used with her clients.

"Look, I'm sorry. It's been a long night. I had two connector flights from Santa Cruz and an hour's drive from Idaho Falls to get here and I'm afraid I'm not at my best. May I come in so we can discuss what's to be done about our runaway parents?"

She wasn't sure how he would have answered if the cell phone clipped to his belt hadn't suddenly bleeped.

With a grim glare—at her or at the person waiting on the other end of the line or at the world in general, she didn't know—then gestured for her to come inside.

"Yeah?" he growled into the phone as the toddler in his arms wiggled and bucked to get down. Wade Dalton let the boy down, busy on the phone discussing in increasingly heated tones what sounded like a major problem with some farm machinery. She caught a few familiar words like *stalling out* and *alternator* but the rest sounded like a foreign language.

"We don't have a choice. The baler's got to be fixed today. That hay has to come in," he snapped.

While she listened to his end of the conversation about various options for fixing the recalcitrant machine, Caroline took the opportunity to study Wade Dalton's home.

Though the ranch house had soaring ceilings and gorgeous views of the back side of the Tetons, it was anything but ostentatious. The furniture looked comfortable but worn, toys were jumbled together in one corner, and the nearest coffee table was covered in magazines. An odd assortment of circulations, too, she noticed. Everything from *O*—Marjorie's, she assumed—to *Nick Jr.* to *Farm & Ranch Living*.

The room they stood in obviously served as the gathering place for the Dalton family. Cartoons flickered on a big-screen TV in one corner and that's where the little blond toddler had headed after Wade had set him down. She watched him for a moment as he picked up a miniature John Deere and started plowing the carpet, one eye on the screen.

The older boy had vanished. She only had a moment to wonder where in the big house he'd gone when Wade Dalton hung up the phone.

"Sorry. Where were we?" he said.

"Discussing what's to be done about our parents, I believe."

"As I see it, we don't have too many options. It's too late to go after them. I'm assuming they left about midnight, which means they've got a nine-hour head start on us. They'd be married long before we even made it to the Nevada state line. Beyond the fact that I can't leave the ranch right now, I wouldn't know where the hell to even start looking for them in Reno since my mother's not answering her cell phone."

"Neither is Quinn," Caroline said glumly.

"I can't believe Marjorie would do something like this, just run off and leave the kids. This is your doing."

So much for their thirty-second ceasefire. "Mine?"

"You're the one who's been telling her to reach for her dreams or whatever the hell other nonsense you spout in your sessions with her."

"You don't thinking reaching for dreams is important?"

"Sure I do. But not when it means walking away from your responsibilities."

"Since when are *your* children your mother's responsibility?" she snapped.

Again she had to force herself not to step back from the sudden fury in his eyes. She had to admit she deserved it this time.

"That was uncalled for. I'm sorry," Caroline said quietly. "Marjorie has been caring for Nat and Cody and Tanner for two years. She doesn't see it as a burden at all."

"Right. That's why she's been paying a small fortune to some stranger so you can tell her all the things wrong with her life and how to fix them."

"That's not what I do at all," she insisted. "I try to help my clients make their lives happier and more fulfilling by pointing out some of their own self-destructive behavior and giving them concrete steps toward changing what they're unhappy about. Marjorie was never unhappy about you and your children."

Before she could continue, his phone bleeped again. He ignored it for four rings, then muttered an oath and picked it up.

This conversation was similar to the first, only Wade Dalton seemed to grow increasingly frustrated with each passing second.

"Look," he finally said angrily, "just call the tractor supply place in Rexburg and see if they've got a replacement, then you can send Drifty over to pick it up. I'll be out as soon as I can. If we put the whole crew out there this afternoon, we might still be able to get the hay in before the rain."

He hung up and then faced her again. "I don't have time to get into this with you today, Ms. Montgomery. I'm sorry you came all this way for nothing but I think we're too late to do anything about the two lovebirds. I'll warn you, though, that if your father thinks he's going to touch a penny of the income from this ranch, you're both in for one hell of a fight."

"Warning duly noted," she said tightly, wondering how a woman as fun and bubbly as Marjorie could have such an arrogant jerk for a son, no matter how gorgeous he might be.

She should cut him some slack, Caroline thought as she headed for the door. He obviously had his hands full, a widower with three active children and a busy cattle ranch.

Just as she reached the door, an acrid scent drifted from the back of the house, stopping her in her tracks.

"Do you smell something?" she asked Wade Dalton.

"It's a working ranch. We've got all kinds of smells."

"No, this is different. It smells like something's on fire."

He sniffed the air for a second, then his eyes narrowed. He looked around the gathering room, his eyes on his youngest son still playing on the carpet and the notable absence of the older boy.

"Tanner!" he suddenly roared. "What are you doing?"

"Nothing!" came a small, frightened-sounding voice

from the rear of the house. "I'm not doin' anything. Anything at all. Don't come in the kitchen, Daddy, okay?"

Wade closed his eyes for half a second then took off down a hallway at a fast run.

This wasn't any of her business, she knew, but Caroline had no choice but to follow.

Chapter Two

Hot on Wade Dalton's worn boots, Caroline had a quick impression of a large, old-fashioned kitchen painted a sunny yellow with a professional-looking six-burner stove, long breakfast bar and at least eight bow-backed chairs snugged up against a massive, scarred pine table.

She imagined under other circumstances it would be a pleasant, welcoming space, but just now the room was thick with black smoke and the acrid smell of scorched paper and something sickly sweet.

Flames shot up from the stove and she quickly realized why—a roll of paper towels was ablaze next to the gas burner and already flames were scorching up the cabinets.

Even more worrisome, the older of Wade Dalton's sons was standing on a chair he must have pulled up to the stove and his SpongeBob SquarePants pajamas were perilously close to the small fire.

"I'm sorry, Daddy," the boy sniffled.

"Get down right now!" Wade yelled in that no-argument parental tone reserved for situations like this.

Though she sensed the rancher's harshness stemmed from fear for his son's safety, his words and tone still seemed to devastate the boy into inaction. He froze on his precarious perch until his father had to lift him off the chair and set him on the floor so he could get close enough to assess the cabinets.

Wade picked up the burning mess of towels and dropped them into the sink then returned to survey the damage.

Still, the boy didn't move, standing as if he didn't quite know what was happening. He looked ill, almost shocky, and he stood directly in Wade Dalton's path.

This wasn't any of her business, Caroline reminded herself. Even as she thought it, she found herself moving toward the distraught little boy.

What was his name? Tucker? Taylor? *Tanner.* That was it. "Tanner, why don't we get out of your daddy's way and let him take care of things here, okay?"

He looked at her blankly for a moment, then slipped his hand in hers and let Caroline lead him from the room. She took him into the great room where his little brother was still busy with his trucks, unaffected by the drama playing out in the other room.

She was going to ask if he had a favorite television show she could find for him as a distraction when she noticed his left hand pressed tightly to his pajama top.

A grim suspicion seized her and she leaned down. "Tanner, can I take a look at your hand? Are you hurt?"

His chin wobbled for a moment, then he nodded slowly and pulled his hand away from his chest. He made a small sound of distress when he spread out his fingers—and no wonder.

Caroline gasped at the angry, blistering red splotch covering his palm, roughly twice the size of a quarter. "Oh, honey!"

Her reaction seemed to open the floodgates of emotion. Tears pooled in his huge blue eyes and rolled over pale cheeks. "I didn't mean to start a fire. I didn't mean to! I just wanted to roast marshmallows like me and Nat and Grandma did with Uncle Seth when we went campin'. Do you think my daddy will be mad at me?"

She thought that was a pretty good bet. Wade Dalton seemed mad at the entire world, as a matter of course. How would he treat his son, angry or not? That was the important thing.

"I'm sure he'll just be worried about you," she assured Tanner, though she wasn't at all convinced of that herself.

"He's gonna be so mad. I'm not supposed to be in the kitchen by myself." His tears were coming faster now and she knew she had to do something quick to head them off or he would soon be in hysterics. Action seemed the best antidote.

"Let's just get your hurt taken care of and then we'll worry about your dad, okay?"

He nodded and Caroline thought quickly back to her thin and purely basic knowledge of first aid.

"We need to put some cold water on that," she told

Tanner, her mind trying to dredge old lessons she'd learned as a girl. "Do you think you can show me a bathroom?"

"Yeah. There's one right through those doors."

She led him there quickly and filled the sink with cold water, then grasped his wrist and immersed it in the sink, though he wasn't keen on the idea.

"I don't want to," he said, sniffling. "It hurts."

"I know, honey. I'm sorry to make you hurt more but this way we can be sure the burn stops."

"Tannoh owie?"

Caroline looked down and found the youngest one had followed them into the small bathroom. Within fifteen seconds, she wasn't sure what held more interest to him—his brother's owie or the lid of the toilet, which he repeatedly flipped up and down with a nerve-racking clatter each time.

Her repertoire of distractions was severely limited but she thought maybe she could tell him a story or something, just to keep him away from the toilet and away from his brother.

"Hey, kiddo," she began.

"His name is Cody," Tanner informed her, his sniffles momentarily subsiding. "He's two and I'm five. I just had a birthday."

"Five is a fun age," she started, but her words were cut off by a loud and angry voice from outside the room.

"Tanner Michael Dalton! Where are you? Get in here and help me clean up the mess you made!"

Caroline took an instinctive step closer to the boy. What a disagreeable man, she thought, until she remembered that he likely knew nothing about his son's injuries.

"We're in the bathroom," she called down the hall. "Do you think you could come in here for a moment?"

Silence met her request for a full five seconds, then Wade spoke in an annoyed-sounding voice. "What is it? I'm kind of in the middle of something here."

Suddenly there he was in the doorway, two hundred pounds of angry male looking extremely put-upon, as if she'd pulled him away from saving the world to ask his opinion on what shade of lipstick to use.

This was his own son and she wouldn't let him make her feel guilty for her compassion toward the boy. Caroline tilted her chin up and faced him down.

"We're in the middle of something, too. Something I think you're going to want to see."

He squeezed into a bathroom that had barely held Caroline and two young boys. Throw in a large, gorgeous, angry rancher and the room seemed to shrink to the size of a tissue box.

"What is it?" he asked.

She pointed to Tanner's soaking hand, a vivid, angry red, and watched the boy's father blanch.

He hissed an oath, something she gauged by Tanner's surprised reaction wasn't something the boy normally heard from his father.

She had to admit, the shock and concern on Wade's features went a long way toward making her more sympathetic toward him.

"Tanner!" he exclaimed. "You burned yourself?"

"It was an accident, Daddy."

"Why didn't you say something?"

Tanner shrugged his narrow shoulders. "I was trying to be a big boy, not a b-baby."

The sympathy from his father was apparently more than Tanner's remarkable composure could withstand. The boy's sniffles suddenly turned to wails.

"I'm sorry, Daddy. I'm sorry. I won't do it again. I *won't,* I promise. It hurts a lot."

Wade picked up his son and held him against his broad, denim-covered chest. "Okay, honey. Okay. We'll take care of it, I promise. We'll find your Uncle Jake and he'll fix you right up."

Cody looked from his crying brother to their father's obvious concern and started wailing, from fear or just sympathy, Caroline wasn't sure. Soon the small bathroom echoed with loud sobs.

After a moment of that, Wade's eyes started to look panicky, like he'd just found himself trapped in a cage of snakes—except she had the feeling he would have preferred the snakes to two bawling kids.

Finally Caroline took pity on him and picked up the crying toddler. He was heavier than she expected, a solid little person in a Spider-Man shirt. "You're okay, sweetie. Your brother just has an owie."

The curly blond cherub wiped his nose with his forefinger. "Tan-noh owie."

"Yep. But he'll be okay, I promise."

"Uncle Jake will make it all better," Wade said, a kind of desperate hope in his voice. "Come on, let's go find him."

He led the way out of the room. Once free of the bath room's confining space, Caroline could finally make her brain function again. She considered the ability to once more take a breath a nice bonus.

Wade carried Tanner toward the front door and she followed with the younger boy in her arms.

"Look, you're going to have enough on your hands at the clinic," she said. "Why don't I stay here with Cody while you take care of Tanner?"

It took a second for Wade's attention to shift from his injured son to her, something she found rather touching—until she saw suspicion bloom on his features.

"No. He can come with us to the clinic."

"Are you sure? I don't mind watching him for you."

She didn't need to hear his answer—the renewed animosity in his eyes was answer enough. "Lady, I don't know you from Adam," he snapped. "I'm not leaving my son here with you."

"Would you like me to come with you and then watch him in the clinic while you're occupied with Tanner's hand?"

He frowned, obviously annoyed by her persistence. Good heavens, did he think she was going to kidnap the child?

"No. He's fine with me. I'm sure there's somebody in Jake's office who could watch Cody while we're in the exam room."

With Tanner in one arm, he scooped up the toddler in the other and carried both boys out the door, toward a huge mud-covered silver pickup truck parked in the circular driveway.

Not sure what to do next, Caroline stood on the broad porch of the ranch house and watched as he strapped both boys into the truck. Wade seemed to have forgotten her very existence. In fact, a moment later he climbed into the driver's seat and drove away without once looking back at the house.

Now that the first adrenaline surge from the fire and dealing with Tanner's burn had passed, Caroline was aware of a bone-deep exhaustion. She had almost forgotten her long night of traveling and the worry over Quinn's whirlwind romance with one of her clients. Now, as she stood alone on the ranch house porch with a cool October wind teasing the ends of her hair, everything came rushing back.

Since she was apparently too late to stop her father from eloping with Marjorie, she should probably just drive her rental back to the airport and catch the quickest flight to California.

On the other hand, that kitchen was still a mess, she was sure. She could scrub down the smoke-damaged kitchen while Wade was gone, perhaps even fix a warm meal for their return.

It was the least she could do, really. None of this would have happened if her father hadn't run off with Marjorie.

She wasn't breaking her vow, Caroline told herself as she walked back into the house and shut the cool fall air behind her. She wasn't cleaning up after her father's messes, something she had sworn never to do again. She was only helping out a man who had his hands full.

She tried to tell herself she wasn't splitting hairs, but even as she went back into the smoke-damaged kitchen and rolled up her sleeves, she wasn't quite convinced.

"There you go, partner. Now you've got the mummy claw of death to scare Nat with when she comes home from school."

Tanner giggled at his uncle Jake and moved his

gauze-wrapped hand experimentally. "It still hurts," he complained.

"Sorry, kid." Jake squeezed his shoulder. "I can give you some medicine so it won't hurt quite so bad. But when you try to put out a fire all by yourself, sometimes you get battle scars. Next time call your dad right away."

"There won't be a next time. Right, Tanner?" Wade said sternly. "You've learned your lesson about roasting marshmallows—or anything else—by yourself."

Tanner sighed. "I guess. I don't like havin' a burn."

Jake straightened. "You were really brave while I was looking at it. I was proud of you, bud. Now you have to be a big kid and make sure you take care of it right. You can't get the bandage wet and you have to try to keep it as clean as you can, okay? Listen to your dad and do what he says."

"Okay." Tanner wiggled off the exam bench. "Can I go ask Carol for my sucker now?"

"Sure. Tell her a big brave kid like you deserves two suckers."

"And a sticker?"

Jake hammed a put-upon sigh. "I guess."

Tanner raised his bandaged hand into the air with delight then rushed out of the exam room, leaving Wade alone with his younger brother.

Unlike old Doc Jorgensen who had run the clinic when they were kids—with his gnarled hands and breath that always smelled of the spearmint toothpicks he chewed—Jake didn't wear a white lab coat in the office. The stethoscope around his neck and the shirt pocket full of tongue depressors gave him away, though.

Wade watched his brother type a few things onto a

slender laptop computer—notes for Tanner's chart—and wondered how the little pest in hand-me-down boots and a too-big cowboy hat who used to follow him around the ranch when they were kids had grown into this confident, competent physician.

This wasn't a life Wade would have chosen, either for himself or for his brother, but he had always known Jake hadn't been destined to stay on the ranch. His middle brother was three years younger than he was and, as long as Wade could remember, Jake had carried big dreams inside himself.

He had always read everything he could find and had rarely been without a book in his hand. Whether they'd been waiting at the end of the long drive for the school bus or taking a five minute break from fixing fence lines, Jake had filled every spare moment with learning.

Wade had powerful memories of going on roundup more than once with Jake when his brother would look for strays with one eye and keep the other on the book he'd held.

He loved him. He just never claimed to understand him.

But there was not one second when he'd been anything less than proud of Jake for his drive and determination, for the compassion and caring he showed to the people of Pine Gulch, and for coming home instead of putting his medical skills to work somewhere more lucrative.

After another few seconds of pounding the keys, Jake closed his laptop.

"Well, I'd tell you happy birthday but it sounds like it's a little too late for that."

Wade made a face. "You can say that again. It's been a hell of a day."

"And just think, it's only noon. Who knows what other fun might be in store."

Wade sighed heavily. Noon already and he hadn't done a damn thing all day. He had a million things to do and now he had a little wounded firefighter who couldn't get his bandage dirty to think about.

His mother ought to be here, blast her. He was no good at the nurturing, sympathy thing. Did she ever stop to consider one of the kids might need her to shower kisses and sympathy?

"So what do you suggest we do about Mom?" he asked.

Jake leaned a hip against the exam table, and Wade thought again how he seemed to fit here in this medical clinic, in a way he'd never managed at the Cold Creek.

"What *can* we do? Sounds like the deed is done."

"We don't have to like it, though."

"I don't know. She's been alone a long time. It's been eighteen years since Hank died and even before that, her life with our dear departed father couldn't have been all roses. If this Montgomery guy makes her happy, I think we should stand behind her."

He stared at his brother. The finest education didn't do a man much good if he lost all common sense. "What do you mean, stand behind her? She doesn't even know the guy! How can we possibly support her eloping with a man she's only corresponded with through e-mail and clandestine phone calls? And what kind of slimy bastard runs off with a woman he's never seen in person? He's got to be working some kind of scam. He and the daughter are in it together."

"You don't know that."

"They've got to be. She trolls for unhappy older women through this life-coaching baloney, finds a vulnerable target like Mom, and then he steps in and charms them out of everything they've got."

"You're such a romantic," Jake said dryly.

"I don't have time to be a romantic, damn it. I've got a national television crew coming to the ranch in six days. How can I possibly get ready for this video shoot when I've got three kids underfoot every second?"

"You could always cancel it."

He glowered at Jake. "You're not helping."

"Why not? It's just a video shoot."

"Just a video shoot I've been working toward for almost a year! This is huge publicity for the ranch. We're one of only a handful of cattle operations in the country using this high-tech data-collection chip on our stock. You know how much of an investment it was for us but it's all part of our strategy of moving the ranch onto the industry's cutting edge. To be recognized for that right now is a big step for the Cold Creek. I don't know why Mom couldn't have scheduled her big rendezvous *after* the news crew finished."

"So what will you do with the kids?"

"I'm still trying to figure that out. You're the smart one. Any suggestions?"

"You could hire a temporary nanny, just until after the video shoot is over. Didn't Mom's note say she'd be back in a week?"

He started to answer but stopped when he heard Cody wailing from the reception area, something about a "stick-oh."

Wade sighed and headed toward the sound, Jake right behind him.

"Right. A week. Let's hope I'm still sane by then."

Cody fell asleep on the six-mile drive from Jake's clinic in Pine Gulch to Cold Creek Ranch. Tanner, jacked up by the excitement of the morning and probably still running on adrenaline, kept up a steady stream of conversation that didn't give Wade a minute to think about what he was going to do.

Tanner didn't even stop his running commentary during the phone call Wade took on his cell from Seth, who informed him glumly that the shop in Rexburg wouldn't have the part they needed for the baler until the next day. Without it, they wouldn't be able to bring the hay in, which meant they might lose the whole damn crop to the rain.

"I'm almost home. I'll get the boys some lunch and then try to come down and see if we can jury-rig something until tomorrow."

The clouds continued to boil and churn overhead as he drove under the arch that read Cold Creek Land and Cattle Company, and Wade could feel bony fingers of tension dig into his shoulders.

Sometimes he hated the responsibility that came from being the one in charge. He hated knowing he held the livelihood of his own family and those of three other men in his hands, that his every decision could make or break the ranch.

He couldn't just take a week off and play Mr. Mom. Too much depended on him meeting his responsibilities, especially right now.

But who could he ask for help? His mind went through everyone he could think of among their neighbors and friends.

His wife's family had sold their ranch a year ago and her parents were serving in South America as missionaries for their church.

Viviana Cruz was the next logical choice. She owned the small ranch that adjoined the Cold Creek to the west and was his mother's best friend as well as a sort of surrogate grandmother to his kids. Unfortunately, she had left the week before to spend some time with her daughter in Arizona before Maggie's national guard unit shipped off to Afghanistan.

He couldn't think of anyone else, off the top of his head. Everyone who came to mind was either busy with their own ranch or their own kids or already had a job.

Seth knew every female with a pulse in a fifty-mile radius. Maybe his brother could think of somebody in his vast network who might be suitable to help with the kids for a week. Though it didn't really have to be a woman, he supposed as he pulled up to the back door of the ranch house.

"Can I watch TV?" Tanner asked when Wade unhooked him from his booster seat.

"Sure. Just no soap operas."

He grinned at the wrinkled-up face Tanner made. "Yuck," the boy exclaimed. "I hate those shows. Grandma watches them sometimes but they're so *boring!*"

By that, Wade assumed he didn't have to worry about Tanner developing a deep and abiding love for drama in the afternoons.

His injury apparently forgotten for now, Tanner

skipped up the steps and into the house, leaving Wade to carefully unhook the sleeping Cody and heft him to his shoulder, holding his breath that he could keep the boy sleep. Cody murmured something unintelligible then burrowed closer.

So far so good, Wade thought as he went inside and headed straight up the back stairs to Cody's bedroom.

This was always the tricky part, putting him into his bed without disturbing him enough to wake him. He held his breath and lowered him to the crib mattress.

Cody arched a little and slid toward the top edge, where he liked to sleep, but didn't open his eyes. After a breathless moment, Wade covered him with his Bob the Builder quilt, then returned downstairs to find Tanner and figure something out for lunch.

He found Tanner in the great room with the TV on, the volume turned low.

"Can you even hear that?" Wade asked.

Tanner answered by putting a finger to his mouth. "Quiet, Daddy. You'll wake up the lady."

Wade frowned. "What lady?"

Tanner pointed to the other couch, just out of his field of vision. Wade moved forward for a better view and stared at the sight of Caroline Montgomery curled up on his couch, her shoes off and her lovely features still and peaceful.

Looked like she had made herself right at home in his absence.

He wasn't sure why the discovery should send this hot beam of fury through him, but he couldn't stop it any more than he could control those clouds gathering outside.

Chapter Three

"Hey lady! Wake up!"

Caroline barely registered the voice, completely caught up in a perfectly lovely dream. She was riding a little paint mare up a mountain trail, the air sweet and clear, and their way shaded by fringy pines and pale quaking aspen. She'd never been on a horse in her life and might have expected the experience to be frightening, bumpy and precarious, but it wasn't. It was smooth, relaxing, moving in rhythm with a huge, powerful creature.

The mountains promised peace, a warm embrace of balance and serenity she realized she had been seeking forever.

"Lady!" the voice said louder, jerking her off the horse's back and out of the dream. "You want to tell me what you're still doing here?"

Jarred, disoriented, Caroline blinked her hazy way back to awareness. Instead of the beautiful alpine setting and the horse's smooth gait beneath her, she was in a large, open room gazing directly at a painting of a horse and rider climbing a mountain trail.

Beneath the painting stood an angry man glowering at her from beneath a black cowboy hat, and it took her sleep-numbed brain a moment to figure out who he was.

Wade Dalton.

Marjorie Dalton's oldest son. In a flash, she remembered everything—Quinn's gushing e-mail about his lady love, her shocked reaction to find his lady love was her client, then that frenzied trip to eastern Idaho in a mad effort to stop him from doing anything rash.

She'd been too late, she remembered. Instead of Marjorie and Quinn, she had found only a surly, suspicious Wade Dalton and his two darling, troublemaking boys.

Striving desperately for composure, she drew in a deep, cleansing breath to clear the rest of the cobwebs from her brain, then sat up, aware she must look an absolute mess.

She pushed a hank of hair out of her eyes, feeling at a distinct disadvantage that he had caught her this way.

"I'm sorry," she murmured. "I didn't mean to fall asleep. I sat down to wait for you and must have drifted off."

"Why?"

"Probably because I traveled all night to get here." To her embarrassment, her words ended in a giant yawn, but the man didn't seem to notice.

"I wasn't asking why you fell asleep. I was asking why in the …" He looked over at his son and lowered his voice. "Why in the *heck* would you think you had to wait for us? As far as I'm concerned, we've said everything we needed to say."

She followed his gaze to the boy, noting the bandage on his hand. "I wanted to make sure Tanner was all right."

"He's fine," he answered. "Second-degree burn but it could have been a lot worse."

"Uncle Jake put lots of stinky stuff on it," Tanner piped up from the other couch, "and said I have to keep it wrapped up for a week 'cept at bedtime, to keep out the 'fection. This is my mummy claw of death."

He made a menacing lunge toward her with his wrapped hand and Caroline laughed, charmed by him.

"You'll have to make sure you do everything your uncle told you. You don't want to get an infection."

"I know." His sigh sounded heartfelt and put-upon. "And I can't ever roast marshmallows by myself again or Daddy will drag me behind Jupiter until my skin falls off."

"Jupiter?"

"My dad's horse. He's really big and mean, too."

Caroline winced at the image and Wade frowned at his son. "I was just kidding about the horse, kid. You know that, right? I just wanted to make sure you know your punishment for playing on the stove again will be swift and severe."

"I know. I told you I wouldn't do it again ever, ever, ever."

"Good decision," Caroline said. "Because you'd look pretty gross without all your skin."

Tanner giggled, then turned back to his television show.

Caroline shifted her attention back to the boy's father

and found him watching her closely, a strange look on his features—an expression that for some reason made her wish her hair wasn't so sleep-messed.

Silence stretched between them, awkward and uncomfortable, until she finally broke it.

"I made some soup for you and the boys. It's on the stove."

He scowled. "You what?"

"I figured you would be ready for lunch when you returned from the clinic so I found some potatoes in the pantry and threw together a nice cheesy potato soup."

She wasn't quite sure why, but her announcement turned that odd expression in his eyes into one she recognized all too well. She watched stormclouds gather in those blue depths and saw his mouth tighten with irritation.

"Funny, but I don't remember saying anything about making yourself right at home." Though his voice was low to prevent Tanner from paying them any attention, it was still hot.

"You didn't. I was only trying to help."

"My mother has apparently been stupid enough to marry your father, but that sure as hell doesn't give you free rein of the Cold Creek, lady."

She inhaled deeply, working hard to keep her emotions under control. No good would come of losing her temper with him, she reminded herself. As far as he was concerned, she had invaded his territory, and his reaction was natural and not unexpected.

At the same time, she couldn't let him minimize her, not when she had only been trying to help.

"My name is Caroline," she said calmly.

"I don't care if you're the frigging queen of England. This is my ranch and right now you're trespassing."

She raised an eyebrow, trying to hang onto her temper. "Are you going to have me thrown in jail because I had the temerity to make you and your boys some soup?"

"The idea holds considerable appeal right about now, believe me!"

Though she knew he was only posturing, dread curled through her just at the possibility of going to jail again. She had a flashing image of concrete walls, hopelessness and a humiliating lack of privacy.

She couldn't bear contemplating that brief time in her life—and couldn't even begin to imagine having to go back.

She took another deep breath, focusing on pushing all the tension out of her body.

"I was only trying to help. I thought perhaps Tanner might need something comforting and warm after his ordeal."

"I don't need your help, Ms. Montgomery. I don't need anything from you. It was the *help* you gave my mother that led to this whole mess in the first place."

Oh, this man knew how to hit her where she lived. First he threatened her with her worst nightmare, then he dredged up all the guilt she'd been trying so hard to sublimate.

Before she could summon an answer, two noises started up simultaneously—his cell phone rang and strident cries started to float down the stairs as Cody awoke.

Wade let out a heavy sigh and rubbed two fingers on his temple. Deep frustration showed on his features and she reminded herself she didn't want to be fighting with him. While she had worked to clean up the sticky, smoky mess in the kitchen, her mind had been busy trying to do the same to the mess her father had created in Wade Dalton's life.

She wanted to think she had arrived at a viable solution.

"I disagree," she said. "I think you do need help. And if you can swallow your anger at me—justified or not—and listen to me, I have a proposal for you."

His glare indicated that the only kind of proposal he wanted to hear from her concerned her plans to leave his ranch, but she refused to let him intimidate her.

He answered his phone just as he headed out of the room to get Cody, now crying in earnest.

When he returned five minutes later, she had Tanner settled at the kitchen table, eating soup with his unbandaged hand and talking her ear off about his trip to the doctor and the stickers he got from his Uncle Jake and how he heard Amber, one of his Uncle Jake's nurses, talking about how his Uncle Seth was the sexiest man in the county.

This Seth person sounded like an interesting character, she thought, then she forgot all about him when Wade walked into the kitchen with Cody on his hip. The rancher looked big and powerful and intimidating, and she thought his brother would have to be something indeed if he could possibly be more gorgeous than Wade Dalton.

Not that she noticed, she reminded herself. As far as she was concerned, he was grouchy and unreasonable and determined that everything in life had to go his way or else.

Still, there was something about seeing the sleepy-eyed toddler in his arms, one little hand flung around his father's neck and the other thumb planted firmly in his mouth, that tugged at her heart.

The boy studied her warily until she smiled, then his reserve melted and he gave her a chubby smile in return, which only seemed to deepen his father's scowl.

"Would you and Cody like some soup?" she asked.

Wade would have told her no but his stomach growled at just that moment and he had to admit the soup smelled delicious—rich and creamy, with a hint of some kind of spice he didn't quite recognize.

"I didn't put rat poison in it, I promise."

He didn't like this suspicion he had that she found him amusing somehow. He plain didn't like *her.* Caroline Montgomery was everything that turned him off in a woman. She was opinionated and bossy, and he didn't trust her motives one iota.

Trouble was, he couldn't figure out what she could be after. What kind of woman travels eight hundred miles to find her father, then, when she doesn't find him, sticks around to make soup in a stranger's house?

She took the decision out of his hands by setting a steaming bowl on the table and setting another smaller bowl on the counter to cool for Cody.

He could eat, he thought grudgingly. Breakfast had been a long time ago and he'd been too shocked over that letter from his mother to pay much attention to what he'd been eating.

He set Cody in his high chair and pulled him up to the table next to Tanner, then noticed something else about the kitchen. It gleamed in the afternoon sunlight shining in through the big windows.

The place had been a mess when he'd left to take

Cody to the clinic, with scorch marks on the walls and a sticky marshmallow goo on the stove. All that was gone.

"You cleaned up." The statement came out more like an accusation than he'd intended but she only smiled in response. He noticed as she smiled that one of her eyeteeth overlapped the tooth next to it just a bit. It was a silly thing but he felt a little of his irritation with her ease at the discovery of that small imperfection.

"I figured you had enough on your hands right now. It was the least I could do anyway. If you hadn't been distracted yelling at me..." her voice trailed off and she flashed that crooked little smile again. "Excuse me, if you hadn't been talking to me in a loud and forceful voice, you probably would have been able to keep a closer eye on Tanner and he might not have had the opportunity to injure himself."

"He would have found a way," Wade muttered. "That kid could find trouble in his sleep. He's a genius at it."

"He does have a lot of energy but he seems very sweet. They both do."

"Sure, while they're busy eating," Wade muttered, then felt like a heel complaining about his own kids.

"Which you should be doing," she pointed out.

Right. He didn't like bossy women, he reminded himself. Even if they had cute smiles and smelled like vanilla ice cream.

Still, he obediently tasted the potato soup his boys were enjoying with such relish, then had to swallow his moan of sheer pleasure. It was absolutely divine, thick and creamy, and flavored with an elusive spice he thought might be tarragon.

Tanner and Cody were carrying on one of their conversations, with Tanner yakking away about whatever he could think of and Cody responding with giggles and the occasional mimicry of whatever his brother said, and Wade listened to them while he savored the soup.

After he had eaten half the bowl in about a minute and a half, Caroline spoke up. "I know Marjorie helped you take care of your children. Do you have someone else to turn to now that she's gone?"

He swallowed a spoonful of soup that suddenly didn't taste as delectable. "Not yet. I'll figure something out."

Before she could answer, Tanner burped loudly and he and Cody erupted into hysterical laughter.

"Hey, that wasn't very polite," Wade chided, even as he saw that Caroline was hiding a smile behind her hand. "Apologize to Ms. Montgomery."

"Nat says that's how people in some places say thank you when their food is real good."

"Well, we're not *in* one of those places. On the Cold Creek, it's considered bad manners."

Cody suddenly burped, too, something Tanner apparently thought was the funniest thing in the world.

"See? Now look what you're teaching your little brother. Apologize to Ms. Montgomery."

"Sorry," Tanner said obediently, even though he didn't look the slightest bit sincere.

"Sowwy," Cody repeated.

"Can we go play now? We're all done."

Wade washed their faces and hands—well, Cody's hands and Tanner's unbandaged one— then pulled Cody down from his high chair and set him on the floor.

"Remember to be careful," he told Tanner, who nodded absently and headed out of the kitchen after his brother.

"It doesn't look like his injury is slowing him down much," Caroline observed.

He sighed. "Not much slows that kid down."

"So what will you do with them while you work?" she asked again.

"I'll figure something out," he repeated.

She folded her hands together on the table and he noticed her nails weren't very long but they were manicured and she wore a pale pink nail polish. He wasn't sure why he picked up on that detail—and the fact that he did annoyed him, for some reason.

"I'd like to volunteer," she said after a moment.

He stared at her. "Volunteer for what?"

"To help you with your children." She smiled that crooked smile again. "I'm self-employed and my schedule is very flexible. I happen to have some free time right now and I'd like to help."

What the hell was her game? he wondered. "Let me get this straight. You're offering to babysit my kids while your father and my mother are off honeymooning in Reno."

"Yes."

"Why would you possibly think I'd take you up on it?"

She slanted him a look. "Why not?"

"Because you're a stranger. Because I don't know you and I don't trust you."

"I can understand your hesitation. I wouldn't want a stranger caring for my children, if I had any. But I can give you references. I was a nanny in Boston for two years while I finished college. I've had plenty of experience with children of all ages and with cooking and cleaning a house."

Did she actually think he would consider it? "Absolutely not."

"Just like that? You won't even think about it?"

"What's to think about? If you were the parent here, would you leave your kids in the care of a total stranger?"

"Probably not," she admitted. "But if I were in great need, I might consider it after I checked out the stranger's references."

His cell phone rang again before he could answer. One of these days he was going to throw the blasted thing out the window.

He saw Seth's number on the caller ID and sighed. "Yeah?" he answered.

"Where the hell are you? You said you'd be down." Seth sounded as frustrated as Wade felt.

"I'm working on it."

"Those clouds aren't moving on. In another hour we're going to be drenched and lose the whole crop. I was thinking I ought to call Guillermo Cruz and see if we can borrow the Luna's baler."

The Rancho de la Luna was the owned by their closest neighbor, Viviana Cruz. Though a much smaller operation than the Cold Creek, Guillermo Cruz kept his sister-in-law's equipment in tip-top shape.

It was a good solution, one he would have thought of if he wasn't so distracted with the kids. "Yeah, do that," he told Seth. "I'll be down as soon as I can. Maybe I can throw together something to fix the other one temporarily. If we can get two machines running out there, we might have a chance."

He hung up to find Caroline Montgomery watching him carefully.

"As I see it, you don't have too many other choices, Mr. Dalton," she said quietly. "Tanner is going to need pampering with that burn of his, at least for a few days, and it needs to be kept free of infection. You can't just lug him and Cody around the ranch with you where the two of them could get into all kinds of things without proper supervision. And by the sounds of it, your plate is pretty full right now."

"Overflowing," he agreed tersely. "Your father picked a hell of a time to take a bride."

She winced and for a moment there he thought she almost looked guilty before her features became serene once more. "I'm sorry. I understand you don't want me here but for the children's sake, at least let me help for a day or two until you come up with another arrangement. I've come all this way for nothing, I might as well make myself useful."

He rubbed the ache in his temple again, the weight of his responsibilities cumbersome and heavy.

What would be the harm in letting her help for a day or two? Her presence would take considerable pressure off him and it *would* be better for the boys to have more diligent supervision than he could provide.

She was a virtual stranger but, like it or not, she was connected to him now by virtue of their parents' hasty marriage.

Anyway, the work he had to do the next few days was close enough to the ranch house that he could keep an eye on her.

That might not be such a bad thing, he thought. If she

and her father were cooking some kind of scam together, he might have some advantage in the long run by keeping his eyes open and knowing just who he was dealing with.

Hank Dalton had had an axiom for cases just like this. *Keep your friends close and your enemies closer.*

What better way to keep her close than by having her right here in his own home?

A stiff gust suddenly rattled the kitchen windows and he watched the clouds dance across the sky as he tried to calculate how much more they would have to pay for feed during the winter if they didn't get the hay in before that storm hit.

"You're right. I don't have too many options right now. I, uh, appreciate the offer."

The words rasped out of his throat as if they were covered in burrs, and she gave him an amused look, as if she sensed how hard they were for him to say.

He really didn't like being such a ready source of amusement for her, he decided.

"Where are your reference phone numbers?" he growled.

She looked at him for a moment, then scribbled some names and phone numbers on a memo sheet off a pad by the phone. Wondering if he was crazy, he grabbed them and stalked to his ranch office off the kitchen.

Ten minutes later he returned. He'd only been able to reach someone at one of the numbers, a woman by the name of Nancy Saunders. He knew it could be a set-up, that she could be part of the con, but at this point he didn't have any choice but to trust her words. She had raved about Caroline's care for her two children a dozen years earlier, about how they'd stayed in touch over the years and she considered Caroline one of the most responsible people she'd ever met.

He didn't want to hear any of this, he thought. He wasn't buying half of it but decided he would be close enough to the house that he could keep an eye on her.

He returned to the kitchen and found her cleaning up the few lunch dishes.

"Did I pass?"

"For now," he muttered. He grabbed his hat off the hook by the back door and shrugged back into his denim work coat.

"Natalie comes home on the bus about three-thirty and she can help you with the boys and with dinner. The freezer's full of food. I don't know what time I'll be in—probably after dark. You and the kids should go ahead and eat, but my mother usually leaves a couple of plates in the fridge for me and for Seth."

"Your brother."

"Right. He's second in command on the ranch and lives in the guesthouse out back, though he usually takes his meals here at the house with the family."

"What kind of food do you like?"

"Anything edible." He headed for the door, anxious to be gone. He stopped only long enough to scribble his cell number on the pad by the phone. "You can reach me at that number if you need anything."

He hurried for his truck, trying his best to ignore the little voice in his head warning him he would regret letting Caroline Montgomery into their lives.

* * *

Through the kitchen window, Caroline watched Wade hurry to his truck as if he were being chased by an angry herd of bison.

She still couldn't quite believe he had actually agreed to her offer. She hadn't really expected him to take her up on it, not with the animosity that had crackled and hissed between them since she'd arrived at the Cold Creek.

He must, indeed, be desperate. That's the only reason he would have agreed to leave his children in her care.

The man wasn't at all what she had expected, and she wasn't sure what to think of him. So far, he had been surly and bad tempered, but she couldn't really blame him under the circumstances.

He intrigued her, she had to admit. She couldn't help wondering what he was like when he wasn't coping with an injured child, a runaway mother and various ranch crises.

She was intrigued by him *and* attracted to him, though she couldn't quite understand why. Something about his intense blue eyes and that palpable aura of power and strength thrummed some heretofore hidden chord inside her.

Big, angry men weren't at all her cup of tea. Not that she really knew what that cup of tea might be—and heaven knew, she'd been thirsty for a long time. But her few previous relationships had been with thoughtful, introspective men. An assistant professor in the history department at the university in Santa Cruz had been the last man she'd dated and she couldn't imagine any two men more different.

Still, there was something about Wade Montgomery….

What had she gotten herself into? she wondered as she set the few dishes from lunch in a sink full of soapy water and went in search of the boys. Or more precisely, what had Quinn dragged her into?

Here she was falling back into old patterns, just hours after she'd sworn that self-destructive behavior was behind her.

She had vowed she was done trying to clean up after Quinn. The only thing she'd ever gotten for her troubles was more heartache. The worst had been those four months she'd spent in jail in Washington state after Quinn had embroiled her in one of his schemes.

Even though she'd had nothing to do with any of it, had known nothing about it until she'd been arrested, she had been the one to pay the price until she had been cleared of the charges.

Even then she couldn't bring herself to sever all ties with her father. Ironic, that, since she frequently counseled her clients to let go of harmful, destructive relationships.

Quinn wasn't really destructive, at least not on purpose. He loved her and had done his best to raise her alone after her mother had died when she was eight. But she was weak when it came to him and she felt like she had spent her entire life trailing behind him with a broom and dustpan.

This time was different, she told herself. This time, three innocent children had been affected by Quinn's heedless behavior. His impulsive elopement with Marjorie had totally upset the balance and rhythm of life here at 11 Cold Creek.

She knew from her coaching sessions with Marjorie that the older woman had been the primary caregiver to her three grandchildren since Wade's wife had died two years earlier.

Marjorie hadn't minded that part of her life and had loved the children, but she'd been lonely here at the ranch and hungered to find meaning beyond her duties caring for her son's children.

Though intellectually Caroline knew she wasn't responsible for Marjorie's loneliness, for Quinn's apparent flirtation that had deepened and become serious, she still felt guilty.

If not for her connection to Marjorie, the two would never have met, and Marjorie would have been home right now caring for her grandchildren.

Caroline had no choice but to help Wade in his mother's absence. It was the decent, responsible thing to do.

Chapter Four

By the time three-thirty rolled around, Caroline had no idea how Marjorie possibly kept up with these two little bundles of energy.

She was thirty years younger than her client and already felt as limp as a bowl of day-old linguine from chasing them around. Between keeping track of Cody, who never seemed to stop moving, and trying to entertain a cranky, hurting Tanner, she was quickly running out of steam and out of creative diversions to keep them occupied.

They had read dozens of stories, had built a block tower and had raced miniature cars all over the house. They'd had a contest to see who could hop on one foot the longest, they'd made a hut out of blankets stretched across the dining table and, for the last half-hour, they had been engaged in a rousing game of freeze tag.

Who needed Pilates? she thought after she'd finally caught both boys.

She had to think Tanner could use a little quiet time and, heaven knew, she could.

"Guys, why don't we make a snack for your sister when she comes home from school?"

"Can I lick the spoon?" Tanner asked.

"That depends on what we fix. How about broccoli cookies?"

Tanner made a grossed out face that was quickly copied by his brother. They adjourned to the kitchen to study available ingredients and finally reached a unanimous agreement to make Rice Krispies squares.

They were melting the marshmallows in the microwave when the front door opened. Caroline heard a thud that sounded like a backpack being dropped, then a young girl's voice.

"Grandma. Hey Grandma! Guess what? I got the highest score in the class on my math test today! And I did my book report on *Superfudge* but I only got ninety-five out of a hundred because Ms. Brown said I talked too fast and they couldn't understand me."

That fast-talking voice drew nearer and, a moment later, a girl appeared in the doorway, her long dark hair tangled and her blue eyes narrowed suspiciously.

"Who are you? Where's my grandma?" she asked warily.

Rats. Hadn't Wade told her about Marjorie and Quinn?

"This is Care-line," Tanner announced. "She can make a block tower that's like a thousand feet high."

It was a slight exaggeration but Caroline decided to let it ride. "Hi. You must be Natalie. I'm Caroline Montgomery. I'm helping your dad with you and your brothers for a couple of days."

"Where's my grandma?" Natalie asked again, her brows beetled together as if she suspected Caroline of doing something nefarious to Marjorie so she could take her place making Rice Krispies squares and chasing two nonstop bundles of energy until her knees buckled.

Caroline wasn't quite sure how to answer. Why hadn't Wade told her about her grandmother's marriage? Did he have some compelling reason to keep it from the girl? She didn't want to go against his wishes but she really had no idea what those wishes were.

Finally she equivocated. "Um, she went on a little trip with a friend."

"Hey look, Nat. I have the mummy claw of death," Tanner climbed down from his chair and shook his arm at her.

"What did you do this time?" Nat asked.

"I burned me when I was roasting marshmallows on the stove. I only caused a little fire, though. Uncle Jake put yucky stuff on it and wrapped it up. Do you want to see it?"

She made a face. "You're such a dork," the girl said.

Tanner stuck his tongue out at his big sister. "You are."

"No, you are."

Caroline decided to step in before the conversation degenerated further. "Would you like to help us make these? We wanted to make a snack for you. They won't take long."

Natalie frowned. "My grandma always fixes me a peanut butter and jelly sandwich after school."

The truculence in her tone had Caroline gritting her teeth. "I can make you one of those if you'd prefer."

Natalie shrugged. "I'm not really hungry. Maybe later." She paused. "What friend did my grandma go on a trip with? Señora Cruz? She lives next door on the Luna Ranch and she's her best friend."

Caroline debated how to answer and finally settled on the truth. If Wade didn't want his daughter to know her grandmother had eloped, he should have taken the time to tell that to Caroline.

"No. Um, she went with my dad."

Natalie digested that. "Is your dad named Quinn?" she asked after a moment.

Okay, so Natalie apparently knew more about her grandmother's love life than her father had. "Yes. Do you know him?"

Natalie shrugged. "Grandma talked to him a lot on the phone. I got to talk to him once. He's funny."

Oh, her father could be a real charmer, no question about that.

"Where did they go?" Natalie asked.

Here, things grew a little tricky. "You'd probably better ask your dad about that."

"Will they be back by tomorrow?"

"I doubt that."

"But I have a Girl Scout meeting after school. Grandma was supposed to take me. We're making scrunchies. If she's not home by then, does that mean I can't go?"

Blast Quinn for putting her in this position, she thought again. For grabbing what he wanted without considering any of the consequences, as usual. She doubted he had spared a single thought for these motherless children and their needs when he'd charmed their grandmother into eloping with him.

"I can probably take you. We'll have to work out those details with your dad."

"I don't want to miss it," she said. "Grandma and me already bought the fabric."

"We can explain all that to your father. I'm sure there won't be a problem."

Natalie didn't look convinced but she didn't pursue the matter.

The rest of the afternoon and evening didn't go well. Tanner's pain medication started to wear off and he quickly tired of the limitations from wearing the gauze on his hand. He wanted to go outside in the sandbox, he wanted to play with Play-Doh, he even claimed he wanted to wash the dishes, that he *loved* to wash dishes, that he would die if he couldn't wash the dishes.

Caroline did her best to distract him and calm his fractious nerves, with little success. How could she blame him for his testiness? Burns could be horribly painful, especially for a child already off balance by the absence of his grandmother, his primary caregiver.

Cody, the toddler, also seemed to feel his grandmother's absence keenly as bedtime neared. He became more clingy, more whiny. Several times he wandered to the front door with a puzzled, sad look on his face and said "Gramma home?" until Caroline thought her heart would break.

Though she did help with Cody, Natalie added to the fun and enjoyment of the evening by bickering endlessly with Tanner and by correcting everything Caroline tried to do, from the way she added pasta to boiling water to how she made the crust on the apple pie she impulsively decided to make to the shade of crayons she picked to color Elmo and Cookie Monster.

By the time dinner was finished, Caroline thought she just might have to walk outside for a little scream therapy if she heard *That's not how Grandma does it* one more time.

At the same time, Caroline couldn't help but notice the girl never said anything about the way her father did things, only her grandmother. And none of the children seemed to find it unusual that they didn't see their father all evening long.

She had to wonder if this was the norm for them. Poor little lambs, if it was, to have lost a mother so suddenly and then to have a father too busy for them.

The only reference any of them made to their father came when Caroline found a cake in the refrigerator and asked Nat about it.

"Oh! That's my dad's cake. Today is his birthday and we forgot it!"

"I made a present," Tanner exclaimed. "It's in my room."

"Present. Present," Cody echoed and followed after his brother up the stairs.

"Why don't we save the pie for your dad's birthday?" Caroline suggested.

Natalie shrugged. "Okay. But grandma made the birthday cake and she makes really good cakes. He probably won't want any pie."

Caroline sighed but set her crooked-looking pie on the countertop to cool.

Despite Natalie's bossiness, she was a huge help

when it came to following the boys' usual bedtime routine. She even helped Caroline tightly wrap a plastic bag on Tanner's hand so he could have a quick bath.

Her cooperative attitude disappeared quickly once the boys were tucked in their rooms, right around the time Caroline suggested it might be Natalie's bedtime, since by then it was after eight.

"I don't have a regular bedtime." Natalie focused somewhere above Caroline's left shoulder and refused to meet her gaze, a sure sign she was stretching the truth.

"Really?" Caroline asked doubtfully.

The girl shook her head, her disheveled hair swinging. "Nope. I just go to bed when I get tired. Like maybe ten, maybe eleven."

"Hmm. Is that right?"

"Yeah. My grandma doesn't care what time I go to bed. Neither does my dad. He's usually out working anyway. Sometimes I even stay up and watch TV after he comes home and goes to bed."

Natalie said this with a such a sincere expression that Caroline had to hide a smile. She wasn't quite sure how to play this. She didn't want to call the girl a liar. Their relationship was tenuous enough right now. Natalie had made it plain she didn't like the way Caroline did anything, that she wanted her grandmother back. Caroline didn't want to damage what little rapport she'd worked so hard to build all evening.

On the other hand, she certainly couldn't allow the little girl to stay up all night for the sake of keeping the peace.

She pondered her options. "How about this?" she finally suggested. "I've got some great bath soap in my suitcase that smells delicious. You can use some while you take your bath and then I'll let you stay up and watch TV until nine. Does that sound like a deal?"

Natalie agreed so readily that Caroline realized she'd been conned. She could only hope Quinn didn't decide to take his new stepgranddaughter on as a protégé, the willing pupil he had always wanted. The partner in crime Caroline had always refused to become.

The storm that had threatened all afternoon had finally started around seven and Caroline discovered an odd kind of peace watching television with Natalie while the rain pattered against the window.

They hadn't been able to find anything good on TV so after her bath Natalie had put in an animated DVD—one of her grandma's favorites, she'd proclaimed.

If it gave the girl comfort, some connection to her grandmother, Caroline was fine with any movie. Before starting the DVD, Nat dug a couple of soft quilts out of an antique trunk in the corner.

"My mom made these," she said casually.

Caroline fingered the soft fabric, deep purples and blues and greens. "They're beautiful! She must have been very talented. Are you sure we're supposed to be using them?"

Nat nodded. "We use them all the time when we're watching TV. Grandma says it's like getting a hug from our mom every time we wrap up in them and it helps keep her a part of our family to use them instead of putting them away somewhere. That one you have is my dad's favorite."

Her chest ached a little to think of Wade Dalton finding some connection to his dead wife through one of the beautiful quilts she had made.

She pulled it over her and watched the movie and listened to the rain and wondered about this family whose lives Quinn's actions had thrust her into.

She was going to kill him.

Wade glanced at the clock glowing on the microwave in the dark kitchen and mentally groaned. Ten-thirty. He had left a stranger with his children—including a cranky five-year-old with a bad burn—for more than ten hours.

He deserved whatever wrath she poured out on him. He'd had every intention of being back at the house before the kids went to sleep. But since the rain had decided to hold out until dark, they had been able to bale the entire crop, even with their busted baler, and then had had to load it and move it to the hay sheds.

Before he'd realized it, the kids' bedtime had come and gone, and here he was creeping into his own house, tired and aching and covered in hay.

At least they had been able to take care of business before the rain had hit in earnest.

Agriculture had changed tremendously just in his lifetime, with computers and handheld stock scanners and soil sensors that took most of the guesswork out of irrigating crops.

But for all the improvements, he found it humbling that he was just as dependent on the weather as his great great grandfather had been a hundred years ago when he'd settled the Cold Creek.

Caroline probably wouldn't understand all that, though. All she knew was that he'd virtually abandoned his children with a stranger all day.

He'd be lucky if she was still here.

Now that was an odd thought. He didn't want her there. He would have vastly preferred things if she had stayed in California where she belonged. He was unnerved whenever he thought of her in his house, with her soft brown eyes and her vanilla-ice-cream scent and the unwelcome surge of his blood when he was around her.

The kitchen sparkled and smelled like apples and cinnamon, with no trace of the charred marshmallow smell Tanner had left behind. He found a small pile of birthday presents on the table along with a crooked-looking pie that looked divine.

Wade studied the pile, guilt surging through him. The day had been so crazy he hadn't given his birthday much thought at all and certainly hadn't considered that his children might want to share it with him.

They had even made him a pie. Apple, his favorite. His stomach growled—Caroline's delicious soup had been a long time ago—and he wanted to eat the entire pie by himself.

He almost grabbed a fork but stopped himself. He had to face the music first and apologize to Caroline for dumping his kids on her all day.

He actually heard music coming from the great room. That wasn't the music he needed to face but at least it gave him a clue where to find her. He followed the sound, his shoulders knotted with tension at the confrontation he expected and deserved.

In the doorway to the room, he frowned. The menu to a Disney DVD was playing its endless loop of offerings but the room was dark except for the light from the television set. At first he didn't think anyone was in the room, but once his eyes adjusted to the dim light, he saw that both couches were occupied. Nat was stretched out on one and Caroline took the other, and both of them were sound asleep.

He studied them for a moment, noting Nat had pulled out Andrea's quilts. Did she miss her mother as much as he did? he wondered.

She stirred a little but didn't wake when he scooped her up and started to carry her back to her room. She was growing up, he thought with a pang in his chest. She was heavier even than she'd been the last time he'd carried her to bed.

It seemed like only yesterday she'd been a tiny little thing, no bigger than one of the kittens out in the barn. Now she was on her way to becoming a young lady.

Another few years and she'd be a teenager. The thought sent cold chills down his spine. How the hell was he going to deal with a teenaged daughter? He had a hard enough time with an eight-year-old.

He pulled back her comforter and laid her on her bed, then studied her there in the moonlight.

She looked so much like her mother.

The thought didn't have the scorching pain he used to have whenever he thought of Andi, taken from him so unexpectedly. That raw, sucking wound had mellowed over the last year or so until now it was a kind of dull ache. He was always aware of it throbbing there, but the pain and loss hadn't knocked him over for a while.

He turned to go but Nat's voice, gritty with sleep, stopped him by the doorway.

"Daddy?"

He paused and turned around. "Yeah. I'm home now. Go on back to bed, sunshine."

"You never call me sunshine anymore."

"I just did, didn't I?"

She gave a sleepy giggle then rolled over.

He watched for a few more moments to make sure she stayed asleep. He wasn't avoiding Caroline, he assured himself.

Finally, he forced himself to walk back down the stairs to the great room.

His houseguest was also still asleep, with her knees curled up and her hands pillowing her cheek. A lock of hair had fallen across her cheek. He almost tucked it back behind her ear but managed to stop himself just in time.

What the hell was wrong with him? he thought, appalled. It seemed wrong, somehow, to stand here watching her while she slept. She wouldn't appreciate it, would probably see it as some kind of invasion of her privacy. He imagined California life coaches were probably big on things like healthy personal space and respecting others' boundaries.

He had to wake her up, though he was loathe to do it for myriad reasons.

"Ms. Montgomery? Caroline?"

Those incredibly long lashes fluttered and she opened her eyes. She gazed at him blankly for a moment then he saw recognition click in. "You're back. What time is it?"

Here we go. Lecture time. He sighed. "Quarter to eleven."

She sat up and tucked that errant strand behind her ear without any help from him. "My word, you keep long hours."

"Show me a rancher who doesn't and I'll show you

a Hollywood wannabe." He shrugged. "This is a crazy time of year, trying to bring in the last crop of hay for the season and get everything ready for snow."

"The children had a little birthday celebration planned for you. We made a pie and everything. Nat said you don't like pie as much as cake so I guess you have your choice now."

He scratched his cheek. "Did Nat happen to mention I don't like birthdays much at all? And I can't say this one is shaping up to be one of my best."

She smiled a little and he was struck by the picture she made there, with her hair messy and feet bare and her eyes all soft and sleepy.

"You've got an hour left. You should make the most of it."

He had a sudden insane image of pressing her back against that couch cushion and kissing that crooked little smile until neither of them could think straight.

Where the hell did that come from? He could feel himself color and had to hope it was too dark for her to see—and that one of her life-coaching skills didn't involve mind reading.

Wherever the thought had come from, now that he'd unleashed it, he couldn't stop wondering how she would taste, whether her skin could possibly be as soft as it looked.

He wasn't going to find out, damn it. He jerked his mind away from those forbidden waters and answered her.

"My big plans include eating most of that birthday pie and then hitting the sack."

Alone, as he'd been for the last two years.

"What about the children?"

"I guess I could save a slice or two for them."

"They were disappointed that they didn't see you before they went to bed so they could give you your presents."

Because he felt guilty, he responded more harshly than he would have otherwise. "This is a working cattle ranch. The kids understand I have responsibilities. I'll try to see them at breakfast and we can open the presents then."

She opened her mouth and he braced himself for the lecture he was sure would follow, but to his surprise, she closed it again.

"Fine."

The chill in her voice annoyed him, for some reason. He deserved it, he reminded himself, and swallowed what was left of his pride.

"I'm sorry I left you alone with them so long. I should have called or something but we had to work our tails off to get the hay in before the rain hit."

"We were fine. Tanner's hand was hurting before bed so I gave him another dose of his painkiller. I hope that's okay."

"Yeah. I, ah, appreciate your help."

"You're welcome."

"Are you sure you don't mind staying a day or two, until I figure something else out?"

"Of course not. I'm more than happy to help."

He couldn't quite understand why she was so willing to step in and help him but he was too tired and hungry now to figure it out.

"Do you have a spare room I could use while I'm here?" she asked. "I left my luggage in my car because I wasn't quite sure where to put it."

"Oh. Of course. I should have thought of that earlier.

There are two guest rooms on this floor and a couple more upstairs. Of the eight bedrooms in the house, only four are being used right now since Cody and Tanner share."

"Upstairs near the children is fine," she said.

"Go ahead and pick one and I'll go get your luggage and find you."

He came back five minutes later with a single suitcase from her trunk, a laptop case and what he guessed was a makeup bag.

He found her in the room across the hall from his own and he tried not to let his imagination get too carried away with what might happen if he crossed that hall in the night.

"Thank you," she murmured and he could tell by the exhaustion in her voice that she would be asleep in minutes.

"You're welcome. Uh, good night."

He brushed past her on his way out the door and was immediately assailed with the delectable scent of vanilla ice cream and warm, sleepy woman, and it was all he could do to keep from reaching for her.

He was definitely going to have come up with another caregiver solution until Marjorie came back. He wasn't sure he was strong enough to withstand having Caroline Montgomery in his house.

Chapter Five

Caroline had no clue what time the day started on a big cattle operation like the Cold Creek so she decided to err on the side of caution. Her travel alarm woke her at 5:00 a.m. and by 5:30 she stood in the large ranch kitchen with a spatula in one hand and a pencil in the other.

With the coffee brewing, biscuits cooking in the oven and bacon sizzling and popping on the huge commercial stove, Caroline tried to organize her thoughts and make some order out of the chaos that had suddenly become her life.

Quinn's latest escapade and her inevitable efforts to clean up the mess he left behind threatened to wreak havoc with her business. She had phone coaching sessions set up with a half-dozen clients today that she would have to reschedule and a speech she was supposed to give to a woman's meditation group over the weekend would have to be canceled.

The timing was lousy, a complication she could ill afford, but it wouldn't destroy her either. One of the advantages of coaching—one of its big appeals to her when she found herself burning out physically and emotionally in her work counseling abused women at a shelter—was that her schedule could usually be flexible.

Sometimes that flexibility took a little creative time management, though, like now.

She glanced out the window over the sink and saw the sun beginning its slow rise above the mountains. She hadn't done her own meditations and affirmations yet this morning so she turned down the bacon, grabbed her sweater and slipped outside to the deck outside the kitchen.

This area must be Marjorie's handiwork, she thought with a fond smile for her client.

Fall-blooming flowers and herbs filled a variety of containers, from an old metal washtub to a rusted watering can. Several sets of whimsical wind chimes hung from an awning, their music gentle and sweet. Under the awning, protected from the cool breeze, a swing covered in green-striped fabric faced the mountains, a welcoming spot to greet the morning.

She sat on the wide, comfortable swing, enjoying the soft swaying, and looked around the Cold Creek.

She wasn't really sure what she thought of Wade Dalton yet, but one thing she could tell just by looking at his ranch—the man ran a tight ship.

The barns she could see from here were freshly painted, the fences near the house gleamed white in the predawn light and she couldn't see any old farm machinery or junk parts sitting around. Everything was neat and organized.

She watched a light flicker on in a small cedar house twenty yards away and wondered if that was the guest house where Wade's brother lived. She hoped she'd made enough bacon for two hungry men and three children.

The air was sharp with fall but sweet and clear, heavy with moisture from the storm the night before. She drew it deep into her lungs and closed her eyes, mentally taking a broom and dust-pan to all the stress cluttering up her mind.

It took some effort this morning, as she had worried for a long time before she fell asleep about Quinn and Marjorie. That negative energy still flowed through her but she breathed in the sweet mountain air until she could feel herself moving back toward center.

When at last she opened her eyes she could see the promise of day in the pale rim above the jagged Tetons.

Though she had a vague memory of seeing those stunning mountains from the more familiar Wyoming side, she didn't think she'd ever been to Idaho before. How had she and Quinn managed to miss it in their rambling life?

She thought they'd been everywhere as they moved from town to town, her father charming and scamming his way across the country, always after the next big deal.

Please, God, not this time, she prayed silently as part of her meditation. Quinn's intentions toward Marjorie had to be just what they seemed. She couldn't bear thinking he might be cooking up another of his schemes. Her father knew how hard she had worked to build Light the Stars, how very much she cherished the career she had created for herself.

Her success meant everything to her. It was her mission in life, the one thing she had discovered she excelled at.

Knowing how much she loved it and how hard she had worked for her success, would Quinn have risked it all by exploiting her connection with Marjorie for less than altruistic motives?

She couldn't bear thinking of it, not now after working so hard to find serenity this morning. But in her deepest heart, she knew she must suspect it or she wouldn't have dropped everything to come after him. She wouldn't be in a stranger's house right now, cooking his breakfast.

She would be burning his bacon, if she didn't stop woolgathering out here, she reminded herself with a grimace, and slipped back inside the warmth of the house to turn it over.

Ten minutes later, she had a tidy pile of notes and an even bigger pile of bacon strips when Wade Dalton walked into the kitchen.

He must have come right from his shower as his hair was damp, his strong, chiseled features freshly shaved. Her insides quivered a little at the sight but she forced herself to push away the instinctive reaction and offer him a friendly smile.

"Good morning."

He headed straight for the coffee maker. "Didn't expect to see you up this early."

"I wasn't certain what time you started your day and

I wanted to be sure to have breakfast ready. How do you like your eggs?"

His eyes startled, he studied her over the rim of his cup. "Um, scrambled is fine," he said after a moment. "But you didn't have to get up so early just to do that. I'm not completely helpless. I can usually manage to toast a couple pieces of bread."

She grabbed three eggs out of the refrigerator and started cracking them in a bowl.

"I enjoy cooking," she assured him as she poured a splash of milk into the eggs and beat them vigorously. "Besides, I wanted to catch you before you left the house anyway. I have a couple of questions for you."

As she added the eggs to the frying pan, she saw Wade shift his weight and realized he looked less than thrilled at the prospect of conversing with her. "What about?"

"Yesterday was so crazy, with Tanner's burn and everything else, that we really didn't have a great deal of time to discuss your expectations."

"My…expectations?" He seemed uncomfortable with the word, though she wasn't quite sure why.

"What you want from me, as far as the children are concerned."

"Oh. Right. As far as the children are concerned." He paused. "I don't know. Whatever you did yesterday is probably fine."

The day before she'd been flying blindly and she disliked going into a situation unprepared. "Last night before I went to bed I made a list of everything I feel I need to know about the children's schedules and their preferences and daily chores. I thought perhaps we could discuss it over breakfast."

She transferred his eggs to a plate, added several strips of the crispy bacon, a couple of the warm biscuits and some strawberry jam she'd found in the refrigerator.

She set it all on the table at one of the place mats she'd found earlier, along with a pretty matching cloth napkin. Wade studied the place setting with a baffled kind of expression on his face but he finally sat down and took a bite of eggs.

Caroline contented herself with a biscuit, a peach yogurt and a glass of juice and sat across from him at a matching place setting.

"That's all you're having?" he asked. "It looks like you fixed enough bacon to feed the whole county."

She shrugged, a little embarrassed that she'd overestimated what was needed. "I'm not much of a breakfast eater."

The kitchen was quiet and she thought how intimate it was sitting with a man while he enjoyed his breakfast. She found the thought disconcerting and quickly spoke up to divert her attention from how very attractive Wade Dalton was.

"Do you mind if I ask you some questions while you eat?"

"I guess not," he said in a tone that plainly conveyed he didn't think her interrogation would improve his digestion.

She plunged forward anyway. "I suppose some kind of rough schedule is the first thing I need to nail down. What time does Nat need to be ready for the bus?"

He swallowed a mouthful of eggs. "Um, you'll have to ask her when she gets up. I think it's about eight or so but she can be more specific."

Caroline wrote a question mark next to bus pick-up. "And what time does the bus usual bring her home?"

"About three-thirty or so. You're probably going to want to ask her that for more specifics. I'm usually not around when she comes back."

Next to bus drop-off, she wrote 3:30 and then another question mark.

"Natalie told me she has Brownies after school today. I need to know what time she is supposed to be there, how long it lasts and directions to her troop meeting."

"I hate to sound like a broken record but you'll have to ask Nat. She'll know all that."

What do *you* know about your daughter? she wanted to ask but held her tongue. So far she wasn't very impressed by Wade's parenting skills. He had ignored his children completely the day before and now he seemed oblivious to the small routines that made up their lives.

Something of her thoughts must have showed on her face because his expression turned defensive.

"Sorry, but my mother took care of those kind of details."

"All right. I'll ask Natalie. She most likely at least has the name of the troop leader I can call."

She studied her list and wondered whether she'd be able to get *any* information from Wade at all. "I suppose that leaves the boys. It would help me to have some idea of their usual routine. Does Tanner go to preschool?"

"He goes a few days a week but, uh, right off the top of my head I'm not sure what days those are. Nat might be able to tell you that too. Or maybe Marjorie wrote it on the calendar or something."

"I checked there. No luck."

"Well, with his burn and all, he probably ought to just stay home for a while anyway."

"You're probably right."

Wade rose from the table, deciding even if she was a great cook, the fluffy biscuits and crisp bacon weren't worth the price of this awkward conversation. "Thanks for the breakfast but I should be on my way."

"I'm not quite finished. That still leaves Cody. Can you tell me what kind of schedule Cody might be on as far as nap time? Does he nap in the morning or afternoon?"

"Um, afternoon." It was a total guess, judging by what had happened the day before, but Wade decided she didn't have to know that.

How could one small, delicate woman make him feel like such an idiot? he wondered. He didn't much like the feeling that he knew nothing about his own children.

It wasn't true anyway. He might not be up on every single detail but he knew Nat adored horses and Tanner liked helping him fix farm machinery and asked a million questions while they were doing it and Cody enjoyed snuggling with his daddy at the end of the day.

"My mother is the one who kept things running around here." Wade's guilt at his own ignorance made him testy. "She would still be keeping them running if not for you and your Don Juan of a father."

Heat flashed in those huge brown eyes but it was gone so quickly he wondered if he'd imagined it.

"We're all trying to make the best of a less-than-perfect situation, Mr. Dalton."

"You don't need to call me Mr. Dalton in that prissy, annoyed voice. You can call me Wade."

"Wade, then. I've known your children less than

twenty-four hours. I know nothing of their likes and dislikes, their routines, their favorite activities. You're asking me, a total stranger, to jump right in and take care of all these details that you don't know and you're their father!"

He stared her down. "I didn't ask you to do anything. You insisted on staying."

She folded her hand together. "You didn't exactly throw me off the ranch when I offered to help."

Just because something was true didn't make it any easier to swallow. Yeah, he'd taken her help and agreed to let her stay. He hadn't had a whole lot of options. He still didn't.

"I've known *you* less than twenty-four hours but already I know you well enough to doubt you would have gone. You're like a cocklebur, lady. You stick to something and don't let go."

She opened her mouth to respond but before she could, the back door opened and Seth came inside—in search of coffee, no doubt.

He was grateful for the interruption, Wade told himself as he watched Seth spy Caroline. Seth instantly shed his typical morning grouchiness to offer her that slow smile of his that seemed to make every female within a hundred-mile radius sit up and purr.

From the cradle, it seemed as if Seth could charm any female into doing anything he wanted. Wade didn't know he did it, he had just seen it hundreds of times. From the checker at the grocery store to the eighty-year-old church organist, every woman in Pine Gulch adored Seth, probably because he adored them right back.

Usually he found his brother's fascination with the

opposite sex—and their inevitable response—mostly amusing. He wasn't sure why but today it bugged the hell out of him.

"Morning. You must be Caroline." Seth aimed the full force of that killer grin in her direction.

"Yes. Hello."

Just because Wade was annoyed didn't mean he could ignore the manners Marjorie had drilled in them. "This is my brother Seth," he said stiffly. "He lives in the guesthouse out back and is the second in command on the ranch. Seth, this is Caroline Montgomery."

Seth smiled at her again. "I always wanted a baby sister. I just never expected to get a full-grown stepsister as pretty as a columbine. Welcome to the family."

Caroline blinked several times but seemed to soak in the whole load of baloney. "My goodness. Stepsister. I hadn't thought of that."

She slanted a quick look at Wade and he wondered why color was suddenly creeping across her cheeks.

He wasn't sure what annoyed him more—her blush at Seth's teasing or the idea that she might be related to him in any way, shape or form.

"What a crock of sh…sunshine. She's not a step-anything."

"Her dad married our mother. Seems to me that's clear enough."

Seth poured coffee and took a sip, then made an exaggerated sigh of delight. "That is one fine cup of coffee. Somebody who can make coffee like that is just what this family needs."

She shook her head. "It's just coffee. Nothing fancy."

"Not just coffee, trust me. I'm something of an expert

and this is delicious."

"Would you like some breakfast?" Caroline asked. "I'm afraid I overdid it a little on the bacon so you can have as much as you want. There are fresh biscuits, too and I'd be happy to scramble some eggs or make an omelet to go along with it."

Seth grinned. "Beautiful, and she cooks, too. I'd have tried to marry Marjorie off a long time ago if I'd known about all the fringe benefits that would come from having a stepsister."

Her laugh sounded like music and Wade decided he needed to leave before he lost his breakfast.

He stomped up from the table and shoved on his Stetson. "I've got work to do," he growled.

Caroline looked startled. "But what about the rest of my questions about the children?"

"Why don't you ask Seth?" he snapped on his way out the door. "Apparently he's got nothing better to do this morning than sit around flirting with anything that moves."

He slammed the door after him, knowing they were both probably watching him like he'd lost his marbles.

The bitch of it was, he wasn't so sure they'd be wrong.

Chapter Six

Caroline's day improved considerably from its inauspicious beginning, though not at first.

Natalie nearly missed the bus since she insisted it didn't come until 8:05 and instead it showed up ten minutes earlier. She managed to make it, just barely, leaving Caroline with a cranky Tanner, who was hurting and mad at the world for it.

Cody slept in until about nine and woke with soaking wet sheets. She couldn't find anything clean to replace them, so the three of them spent the morning tackling mountains of laundry.

She didn't mind the work—it might have been pleasant except for Tanner's crankiness. He whined when she wouldn't let him have leftover pie for breakfast. He wrapped about half a roll of toilet paper around his other unburned hand so both hands would match. He threw a tantrum when she refused to let him take off his bandages to help her wash dishes.

It was all she could do to remember he was a little boy in pain and in need of comfort.

Cody was a sweetheart but he stuck to her like flypaper and didn't seem to want to let her out of his sight. That was fine since she could always keep an eye on him, but he also managed to find something to make a mess with wherever they were—unmatched socks in the laundry room, flour and sugar in the kitchen, the rest of Tanner's roll of toilet paper that ended up stretched all the way down the stairs.

Worn out by lunchtime, she finally promised the boys a walk after they ate if Tanner agreed to wear a sock over his bandage to protect his hand and keep it clean.

Both boys were thrilled at the prospect of showing her around the ranch, so they ate their peanut-butter sandwiches quickly and even helped her straighten up the Cody mess.

Outside, they found a perfect October afternoon—sunny and pleasant, with just a hint of autumn in the cool breeze and the dusting of bronze on the trees. The storm of the day before seemed to have blown away, leaving everything fresh and clean.

Keeping close watch on Tanner racing eagerly ahead of them, she held Cody's hand and let the toddler's short legs set the pace as she enjoyed the fresh air and the beautiful mountain views.

Up close, the ranch was even more impressive than it had been in the pale early morning light. Everything she saw pointed to a well-run, well-organized operation.

Wade Dalton hadn't sacrificed aesthetics, either.

Instead of what she assumed would be more efficient and inexpensive barbed-wire fences, the ranch had gray-weathered split-rail fence that looked like something out of an old Western movie.

They walked along the fence line down the long gravel driveway toward the main road, stopping to admire a small grazing herd of horses.

"Horse, horse!" Cody exclaimed with glee.

She smiled down at him, charmed by his enthusiasm. "They're pretty, aren't they?"

"See that yellow one?" Tanner leaned on the middle slat of the fence and pointed to a small buckskin pony. "Her name is Sunshine and she used to be Nat's but now she's mine 'cause Nat has a new horse named Chance. I can ride her all by myself. Want to see?"

He started to slip through the rails but Caroline grabbed him by his belt loops. "Not a good idea, bud. At least not until your uncle Jake clears it, okay?"

"But she's my horse! Grandma taught me how to take care of her. She comes when I call her, except she's too big for me to put the saddle and bridle on. Grandma helps me with that part. We ride just about every day."

"Do you go with your dad, too?"

Tanner shrugged. "He's usually too busy."

Too busy to take his son riding? She frowned but before she could say anything, Cody pulled away from her and headed off as fast as his little legs could go. "Hi, Daddy! Hi, Daddy!" he shrieked.

She turned and found Wade coming out of the nearby barn, carrying a bale of hay in each arm like they were feather pillows. He had his jacket off and his sleeves rolled up and she saw those powerful muscles in his arms barely flex at the weight.

Caroline didn't like the realization that her mouth had completely dried up, like an Arizona streambed in the middle of the summer.

Cody collided with his father's legs at a fast run but Wade managed to stay upright. "Hey there, partner. Watch where you're going."

He dropped the bales to the ground as Cody hugged one long leg. Tanner hurried over to his father, too, and hugged the other leg. She was pleased to see he didn't look annoyed at his sons, just distracted.

"Hey Dad, guess what? We're showin' Caroline around," Tanner announced. "I showed her Sunshine and told her she's my very own horse. She is, huh, Dad, 'cause Nat rides Chance now. She says Sunshine is a baby's horse but that's not true 'cause I'm not a baby, am I, Dad?"

He opened his mouth to answer but before he could, Cody tugged on Wade's jeans and held his arms out.

"Daddy, Cody up!"

Wade picked him up and immediately Cody started trying to yank off his hat. Wade held onto his hat with one hand and the wriggling toddler with the other. "I didn't expect to see you guys outside today."

"Caroline says we all needed fresh air and she wanted to see the ranch so we're givin' her a tour. She made me wear a sock on my hand so I won't get a 'fection. That's stupid, huh Dad?"

He looked at the sock then raised an eyebrow. She knew she shouldn't feel defensive but she couldn't seem to help it.

That instinctive reaction gave way to surprise when he shook his head. "Doesn't sound stupid to me, cowboy. I think it's a good idea. Remember what Uncle Jake said—you have to keep it clean."

"I wanted to play in the sandbox but she wouldn't let me do that either," he complained.

"Tough, kiddo. Right now you need to listen to what she tells you. I know it's hard but it would be a whole lot harder if you don't do everything you can to keep your hand clean. If you got an infection, you might even have to have shots and stuff. Caroline is just trying to help you do what Uncle Jake told you. Instead of giving her a hard time, you ought to be thanking her for looking out for you."

She knew it was ridiculous but she still felt a soft, warm glow spread through her at his support of her, and she couldn't contain a pleased smile. He studied her for several seconds and she could almost swear he was staring at her mouth.

Color spread across her cheekbones and she was relieved when Tanner spoke up.

"Hey Dad! Can we show Caroline the kittens?"

"If you promise not to touch them. You'll have to just look today because they might have germs."

"I promise." Tanner took off running. The minute Wade set Cody down, the little boy raced after his brother and the two of them went inside the barn. Caroline followed and was surprised and pleased when Wade accompanied them.

The kittens were right inside the door, in a small pile of hay that looked warm and cozy. She had expected newborns, for some reason, and was surprised to see the half-dozen or so gray and black kittens looked at least a few weeks old.

They wriggled and mewed and climbed all over each other.

"Can Caroline hold one, Dad?" Tanner asked. "She doesn't have a sore hand."

"If she wants to."

"I do," Caroline declared, picking up a soft gray kitten with big blue eyes. "You are darling!" she exclaimed.

"She'll be a good mouser like her mother in a few months."

She made a face at Wade. "I'd prefer to enjoy her like this for now, all cute and furry, instead of imagining her with a dead mouse in her mouth, thanks."

"Whatever helps you sleep at night, I guess."

She laughed and met his gaze over the kitten. He was looking at her mouth again. She could swear it and she didn't quite know what to read into that.

"Any word from the newlyweds?" he asked.

Any glow she might have been foolish enough to briefly enjoy in his company, warm or otherwise, disappeared at his abrupt question and the sudden hard look.

"Nothing," she said. "You?"

"No. I expected them to check in by now. This isn't like Marjorie. Your father doesn't appear to be the best influence on her."

She had to bite back a sharp retort that maybe *Marjorie* was the bad influence on *Quinn*. But since she knew that was highly unlikely—that Wade was likely in the right since Quinn had spent his whole life perfecting the art of being a bad influence—she kept her mouth shut.

"I've tried to call my mother's cell phone at least a half-dozen times this morning. No answer."

"Same goes for Quinn. I guess they've turned them off."

"Probably because they know they've been selfish and irresponsible to run off in the middle of the night."

"Or maybe because they're on their honeymoon and in love and don't want to be disturbed by lecturing children."

She could only hope.

"Right." The skepticism in his voice was plain. "I've got to get back to work."

"Thank you for showing us the kittens." She set the little gray one back with its siblings. "Come on, guys. We'd better head back to the house so we can meet Natalie's bus and get her to Girl Scouts on time."

Both boys were reluctant to leave the fascinating kittens but they obediently walked out into the afternoon sunshine.

"Bye-bye, Daddy," Cody said.

"We're havin' cake and ice cream for your birthday tonight, Daddy, since we missed it yesterday," Tanner chimed in. "Don't forget, okay? We have presents and everything."

Wade looked about as thrilled by that prospect as the boys had been at leaving the kittens. "Is that really necessary?"

"Yep," Tanner said.

"See you at dinner," Caroline said, forcing a smile, then herded her small charges back toward the house.

Wade watched them go, Cody's little hand tucked in Caroline's and Tanner skipping ahead. Why did he suddenly feel so itchy and uncomfortable, like he'd broken open those hay bales and rolled around in them?

He wasn't sure he liked seeing her with his kids. After less than a day, Tanner and Cody both already seemed crazy about her. They sure didn't obey *him* so immediately.

A hundred feet away or so, she stopped abruptly and the three of them bent down to look at something in the dirt—a bug, he'd wager, since the ranch had plenty and Tanner was fascinated with them all.

He looked at those three heads all bent together: Caroline's soft sun-streaked hair, Cody's curly blond locks several shades lighter and Tanner's darker. His chest suddenly felt tight, his insides all jumbled together.

He wanted her. The grim knowledge sat on him about as comfortably as a new pair of boots.

How could he be stupid enough to hunger for a completely inappropriate woman like Caroline Montgomery? He didn't like her, he didn't trust her, but for the first time in two years he felt that undeniable surge of physical attraction to a woman.

Two years. He hadn't been with a woman since Andrea had died—before that, really, since she'd been pregnant with Cody and hadn't felt great the last trimester.

He hadn't even considered it until now, until Caroline had shown up on his doorstep.

Even thinking about this woman he barely knew in the same breath as Andi seemed terribly disloyal and he suddenly missed his wife with a deep, painful yearning.

In the two years since she'd been gone, the first wild shock of unbelievable pain had dulled to a steady, hollow ache except for moments when it flared up again like a forest fire that had never quite been extinguished.

Andi should be the one out there showing bugs to the boys and walking with Cody's little hand tucked in hers and kissing Tanner's owies all better. For a moment, the gross unfairness of it cut at him like he'd landed on a coil of barbed wire.

She'd loved being a mother and she'd been great at it. It was all she'd wanted. She used to talk about it even when they were in high school, about all the kids she would like and how she planned to get a teaching degree first, then wanted to be able to stay home and raise her children.

She'd been two years behind him in school, Andrea Simon, the prettiest girl in the sophomore class. She'd been barely sixteen when they'd gone on their first date and, from that moment, he'd known she was it for him.

He picked up the hay bales and headed for the pens, remembering how sweetly innocent she'd looked at his senior prom. They'd dated on and off while she'd finished high school, though he'd been so busy after his father had died, with all his new ranch responsibilities, he hadn't had much time for girls.

Still, he'd known he loved her from the beginning and he'd asked her to marry him when she was only twenty, on the condition that she finish her education first.

The day after her college graduation, they'd been married in a quiet ceremony in her parents' garden. Marjorie and his brothers had still been living in the ranch house, so Wade had brought his bride home to the little guesthouse out back where Seth lived now.

He could still see Andi's delight in fixing up the place that summer before she'd started teaching at the elementary school in town—sewing curtains, painting, refinishing the floors. While he'd been consumed with the ranch, she'd been building a nest for them.

He cut the twine on the bales and tossed them into the trough, then went back to the barn for a couple more, his motions abrupt as he remembered the heady joy of those early days.

His wife had been his first and only love—and his first and only lover.

Something like that would probably make him look pretty pathetic in the eyes of someone sophisticated like Caroline Montgomery, but he didn't care.

He had loved his wife and would never have dreamed of straying. Their relationship had been easy and comfortable. They had always been able to turn to each other even when hard times had come—the trio of miscarriages she'd suffered in quick succession, the surgery to correct a congenital irregularity in her uterus, then the eighteen months they'd tried without success to become pregnant.

He had lived through the most helpless feeling in the world watching the roller-coaster ride of hope and heartache she'd gone through each month when she realized she hadn't conceived.

And then, three years after they'd married, Andi had become pregnant with Natalie. They hadn't told anyone for nearly half the pregnancy, until well into the fourth month when they'd finally allowed themselves to hope this pregnancy wouldn't end in heartbreak.

Andi had never been happier than she was after Natalie had come along—though with complications—and then Tanner. She'd quit teaching, just as she had dreamed, and had spent her days coloring and singing and looking for bugs on the sidewalk.

He'd been happy because *she* had been happy and they slipped into a comfortable, hectic routine of raising cattle and raising kids.

And then fate had taken her from him and for the last two years he'd done his best to figure a decent way to do both by himself.

He sighed. Why was he putting himself through this today, walking back down a memory lane covered with vicious thorns on every side?

Because of Caroline. Because even though it was crazy and seemed disloyal to Andi somehow, he was attracted to her.

It was only his glands, he told himself, just a normal male reaction to a beautiful woman brought on by his last two years of celibacy.

She was the first woman in two years to even tempt him. He found that vaguely terrifying. He'd had offers at cattle shows and the like, but had always declined the not-so-subtle overtures, feeling not even a spark of interest in any of those women.

Something about their heavy makeup and the wild, hungry light in their eyes turned him off, cheapened something that had always seemed beautiful and natural with his wife.

He had wondered if that part of him was frozen forever. Things had been easier when it had been. But now Caroline had him wondering what it would be like to kiss her, to touch that soft skin. To remember once more the sweet and compelling curves of a woman.

He wasn't going to find out. His mother would be

back soon and everything would get back to normal, to the way it should be without strange women showing up to complicate an already stressful life.

Until then, he would just do his best to get Caroline out of his mind. Hard, relentless work had helped him survive these last two painfully lonely years.

It could certainly help him get through a few more days.

Caroline wasn't sure what to think of a man who was forty-five minutes late for his own birthday party.

"He's not coming, is he?" The resignation in Natalie's voice just about broke her heart.

"He'll be here," Caroline promised, though even as she said the words she questioned the wisdom of raising potentially false hope in the girl.

"No he won't. He's probably too busy. He's *always* too busy."

She shrugged like it meant nothing to her but Caroline only had to look at all Nat had done since her Girl Scout meeting to know her nonchalance was a facade—the festively decorated table, the cake with its bright, crooked frosting and the coned party hats Natalie had made out of construction paper, markers and glitter all told a far different story.

Caroline wanted to find Wade Dalton wherever he was hiding out on his ranch and give the man a good, hard shake.

"I'm hungry," Natalie announced after a moment. "I don't think we should wait for my dad. We should just go ahead and eat since he's not coming."

"I'm hungry, too," Tanner announced.

"Hungry, too," Cody echoed, but whether he meant it or was just parroting his siblings, she didn't know. It didn't much matter anyway. She had three children here who needed their dinner.

"We can wait a few more minutes and then I'll call him to see how much longer he's going to be."

And maybe add a few choice words about fathers who neglect their children, while I'm at it.

The thought had barely registered when they heard the thud of boots on the steps outside and, a moment later, the door opened and a dark head poked through the opening.

A dark head that did not belong to Wade Dalton.

Caroline let out a frustrated breath but her annoyance at finding another man there instead of their father didn't seem to be shared by the children.

"Uncle Jake!"

Pique at her father apparently forgotten for the moment, Natalie shrieked and launched herself at the man. He picked her up with an affectionate hug.

This must be Marjorie's middle son, the family physician, Caroline realized. She studied him as he greeted the children with hugs all around. Jake Dalton was about the same height as Wade but perhaps not as muscular. His hair was a shade or two lighter than Wade's and not quite as wavy, but he shared the same stunning eyes, the same chiseled features.

She could only wonder at the genetics that produced three such remarkably good-looking men in one family. The Dalton gene pool certainly didn't look like a bad place to swim.

While she was studying Jake Dalton, his attention was drawn to the table with its festive decorations and the thickly frosted cake. "Wow. A party for me? You shouldn't have!"

Natalie giggled as he set her back on her feet. "It's not for you. It's supposed to be Dad's birthday party since we forgot it yesterday. Only I bet he's not coming."

"All the more cake for me, then," Jake teased his niece, although Caroline thought for a moment there she saw just a hint of irritation flicker in his gaze.

Did he also notice his brother's careless attitude toward his children? she wondered.

He turned to her and offered a smile she somehow found calming and kind.

"Hello. You must be Caroline. I'm Jake Dalton, Wade's brother. Wade told me you offered to stay on for a few days and help him with the boys. I can't decide if you're insanely nice or just insane."

"A little of both, I guess." She smiled. "Since you're here, why don't you stay for dinner? I was just about to call your brother to see when he's going to make it back."

"I just dropped in to take a look at Tanner's hand but I could probably be convinced to stay and eat."

"And I thought the days of the house call were over."

"I give special service for five-year-old rascals in desperate need of a sucker transfusion." He pulled a lollipop from his shirt pocket and waved it like a magic wand.

She played along. "I only hope you're not too late, Doctor."

"Been that kind of a day, has it?" His expression was both sympathetic and understanding. Dr. Dalton must have a heck of a bedside manner with that calm, competent manner, she thought.

"He's a young boy in pain. A little crankiness is to be expected."

"You're an angel to put up with him. If your father's anything like you, no wonder he swept Marjorie off her feet."

She had spent her entire life trying *not* to be like her father, charming and feckless and irresponsible, but of course she couldn't say that to another of Marjorie's concerned sons.

"He hasn't been too bad, as long as I keep him busy," she said.

"Let's have a look at it, shall we? Climb on up here, cowboy."

Tanner made a face but obeyed his uncle, scrambling up to sit on the breakfast bar.

"Caroline, if you're not too busy with dinner, can you play nurse for a moment?" Jake asked her.

"Of course. Let me wash my hands."

She scrubbed hard then helped Jake as he started unwrapping the bandage. To Caroline, the boy's injury looked red and ugly but Jake smiled. "You're doing great. Everything looks good."

"When can I stop wearing the stupid bandage?"

"Another few days. Maybe a week. You can hang on that long, can't you?"

"I guess." Tanner didn't look thrilled at the prospect, but his uncle told him a couple of knock-knock jokes to take his mind off it while he pulled some ointment from his bag and applied it with gentle care, then put a new bandage on.

While he worked, Caroline couldn't help comparing the three Dalton brothers.

Where Seth had been flirtatious and charming to her at breakfast, the kind of man who knew his own tremendous appeal and reveled in it, in just a few moments Caroline had determined that this middle Dalton brother seemed to be the thoughtful, introspective brother.

That must make their oldest brother the grouchy, unreasonable one.

Her sudden smile drew Jake's attention. "So you're the life coach my mother's been working with."

Her smile turned wary. "Yes," she said, not at all eager for another confrontation with one of the Dalton brothers.

"You must be doing something right. The last few months Marjorie has seemed—I don't know, more centered, focused—than I've ever seen her."

"I don't know how much of that is my influence or how much is from her e-mail romance with my father—a courtship, by the way, that I knew nothing about until yesterday."

Wade didn't believe her but for some reason she felt it important to convince at least one of the Dalton brothers of her innocence.

"A sore spot, is it?"

She hadn't realized how much her professional pride had been stung by Marjorie and Quinn's elopement until just that moment. Until the day before, she had been so pleased with Marjorie's progress in the six months she'd been working with her.

She supposed it was arrogant to think she'd been making a difference in the woman's life, but she had seen her client blossom as she'd started to break free of destructive patterns and take control of her own life.

Now she had to wonder how much of Marjorie's transformation had been due to her coaching and how much was from Quinn's attentions.

Jake was waiting for an answer, she realized. She sighed, checking to be sure the children's attention was occupied elsewhere. Tanner was busy with his lollipop in hand and had wandered over to the refrigerator where Natalie and Cody were busy making words out of alphabet magnets. Natalie was spelling out *horse,* Caroline noted with little surprise.

"Your brother thinks my father and I are running a scam to bilk mature women out of their retirement nest eggs," she finally said.

Jake leaned against the counter and folded his arms. "Are you?"

"Of course not! I have a legitimate business. You can check my Web site with my complete résumé, articles I've written and dozens of client testimonials!"

"You have a masters in social work, spent five years working in the field then graduated from an accredited coaching school. You've had articles published in various women's magazines, have an active affirmation e-mail newsgroup and will soon be publishing a book from Serenity Press on how to tap into the healing energy within. Sounds great, by the way. I'm going to want to order autographed copies since I've got plenty of patients who can use all the healing energy they can find."

She stared at him. "How do you know all that?"

He smiled as he shrugged. "I checked you out months ago when Marjorie started working with you. Wade isn't the only overprotective son in this family. You can find out all kinds of things about a person just by Googling them."

Caroline wasn't sure what to think about this middle son of Marjorie's. Part of her wanted to be offended that he had run a background check on her, but she expected her clients to fully investigate before signing up for her services. She couldn't be annoyed when their family members did the same thing.

How far back did his background check go? she wondered. Her record should have been expunged when she'd been cleared, but he might still find evidence that she'd served jail time while awaiting trial. No, he wouldn't be looking at her with such a friendly smile if he knew about that part of her past.

"You have a solid business," Jake went on, "a healthy reputation and the recommendation of many very satisfied customers. When your book hits the stands, I'm sure you'll have people knocking down your doors wanting your services."

"I've worked hard for what I've earned."

And everything would be ruined if Quinn decided to grift someone he'd found on her client list. But she couldn't let herself worry about that now.

"It shows."

"Apparently not to your brother."

"Wade will come around. He's a hard man but he's not completely unreasonable."

Her doubtful look earned a laugh from Jake but he quickly grew serious again.

"He's a hard man," he repeated. "But he's had to be. He took on the whole responsibility for running the ranch when he was eighteen years old and helped Mom finish raising Seth and me, not an easy job. These last few years since Andi died have been tough in a lot of ways. If he's abrupt and surly, he has reason to be. Don't take it personally."

"Thanks. I'll try to remember that. A doctor who makes house calls and doles out advice, too. You must do a booming business."

"All part of the service."

He smiled and she couldn't help but return it, but before she could respond, she heard a noise and turned to find Wade standing in the doorway.

Hard, indeed. Right now the oldest Dalton brother looked tough enough to chew nails.

Chapter Seven

Wade registered two things when he walked into his kitchen.

The first was the table adorned with balloons and other festive decorations and a birthday cake covered in chocolate icing. His damn birthday party, he remembered. So much for his hopes of grabbing a quick bite to eat and going back to work.

He didn't like the other thing he saw any better. His brother Jake was there, as solemnly handsome as ever. Normally he enjoyed having Jake around but he wasn't thrilled to see Caroline smiling up at his brother in a way she'd never looked at *him*.

His mood darkened further when she caught sight of him and her smile instantly melted away like icicles on a tin roof.

His reaction was irrational, he knew it, but it bugged the hell out of him that she couldn't spare him so much as a tiny smile, when she seemed to have more than enough for his brothers.

He wasn't jealous, he told himself. Just protective of his brothers. Sure, they were grown men, but he didn't need either of them to get tangled up with her until they knew what she and her old man were up to.

Somehow the rationalization rang hollow but it was the best he could come up with.

Before he could give even so much as a terse greeting, the kids caught sight of him.

"Daddy birthday!" Cody exclaimed gleefully. "Birthday, birthday, birthday!"

"You made it!"

Why did Nat have to sound completely astonished? he wondered. "Sorry I'm a little late. The vet showed up an hour ago and we had a few things to take care of."

They weren't close to being done either. Wade had planned just to slip away for a moment to eat and say good-night to the kids, but now he wondered if he ought to tell Dave to come back in the morning.

"That's all right." Caroline's voice was calm but impersonal. "The important thing is that you're here now. The children have been so excited to celebrate your birthday."

"We made you a cake," Tanner said. "It's chocolate. I got to put on some frosting but only if I used my hand that doesn't hurt."

"I bet it's delicious."

"We're having roast beef since I told Caroline it's your favorite dinner," Natalie announced.

Was it? He liked plenty of different foods—anything

put in front of him, usually—and he wasn't quite sure why his daughter thought roast was his favorite.

"Sounds delicious," he murmured.

"We didn't make mashed potatoes, though. I told Caroline that was your favorite but she decided to do a different kind of potato. What's it called again?"

"Twice-baked," Caroline said. For some reason she looked a little embarrassed. "It's a lot like mashed potatoes, just a little fancier."

"Everything smells great. Um, just let me wash some of the dust off and then we can eat."

He would rather have just washed his hands and sat down in all his dirt but he couldn't, not with Jake sitting in there looking so suave and professional and *doctorly* in tan pants and a button-down shirt.

The thought made him wish, conversely, that he had time to shower, but he knew he didn't, not with the vet waiting, so he quickly settled for changing his shirt, combing his hat-flattened hair and washing his face and hands.

On the way back to the kitchen, he called Dave to tell him what was up and invite him for dinner.

"I ate before I came over. Linda's on swing shift this week so we ate before she left for work."

"Well, come on up for cake then," he mumbled, embarrassed all over again about the whole thing.

Dave laughed. "Thanks but I think I'll pass. I've got plenty to keep me busy until you come back down and we can finish up."

"I'll get away as soon as I can," he promised, then disconnected, squared his shoulders, and headed into the kitchen.

Once there, he discovered Seth had come in while he'd been gone, and his younger brother *had* taken time to shower, apparently.

His hair was damp and he looked his usual charming self. He and Jake were both watching Caroline bustle around the kitchen like a couple of fat toms eyeing a nice juicy canary.

He couldn't blame them for it. With that apron and her hair up in some kind of ponytail thing, she looked sexy and rumpled. Her cheeks were flushed, her eyes bright and she had a tiny smudge of what appeared to be chocolate icing on her chin, like a beauty mark.

His sudden desire to reach forward and lick it off just about had him heading right back out of the kitchen.

"Sit down, Daddy," Natalie ordered, in what Andi used to call her lady-of-the-manor tone.

He obliged, taking his place at the head of the table.

"You have to put on your birthday hat," Nat commanded. "Tanner and me made 'em ourselves.

He studied it by his plate, a spangled creation that looked like something a mad magician would wear. A shower of multicolored glitter fell off when he picked it up and he figured he would have rainbow sparkles in his hair for weeks.

Nat, Caroline and the boys all had similar but less gaudy creations on but both his brothers were looking on with bare-headed amusement.

"Why don't you have hats?" he growled.

Seth shrugged, but there was a gleeful look in his eyes that made Wade want to pound something. "You're the birthday boy."

He felt like an idiot but he couldn't disappoint his

kids. With a resigned sigh, he pulled on the creation, snapping his chin with the elastic in the process.

"Let's eat, then," he said.

Caroline had to give credit to Wade for being a good sport.

Though he looked as if he would rather be sitting in church in his underwear, he wore the birthday hat without further complaint all through dinner; he endured the off-key singing of "Happy Birthday" from his children; he suffered through his brothers' jokes on his behalf about his advancing age.

He even made a birthday wish before blowing out the candles on his sagging cake—though if she had to guess, she suspected his wish most likely involved figuring out some way to escape the unwanted attention.

If not for his frequent looks at the clock or the faint, embarrassed expression or the increasingly hard set of his jaw, she might have thought he was even enjoying himself.

He lasted nearly forty minutes before sliding his chair back and removing the birthday hat.

"This has been great, guys. Really. The best thirty-sixth birthday party I've ever had."

Nat made a "duh" kind of face. "It's the only one you've ever had!"

"Well, I'm afraid I have to go," he said. "I can't keep the vet waiting any longer."

Seth stood up. "It's your birthday celebration. Why don't you stay and I can go out and help Dave?"

Caroline saw surprise register briefly on Wade's tanned features at the offer before he shook his head.

"Not this time. We're working out the breeding schedule for next year and it's not something I can miss."

Seth's jaw worked for a moment, but he slouched back down to his seat and reached for his drink, saying nothing.

Did Wade completely miss the sudden restless light in his brother's eyes? she wondered. How could he completely shoot down his brother's offer of help, especially during his own birthday celebration with his children?

The way he ran his ranch *or* his family was absolutely none of her business, she reminded herself as he kissed his children and bid them good-night.

To her shock, before he left the kitchen, he paused beside her chair, looking big and rangy and slightly uncomfortable.

"Thank you for the nice birthday dinner. I can't remember roast beef ever tasting so good and those potatoes were wonderful. It was a lot of trouble to go to and I, um, appreciate it."

She blinked several times but before she could summon a response, he shoved on his Stetson and headed out the door.

"You're welcome," she murmured to his back.

What a complicated, contradictory male, she thought. Just when she thought she had him figured out, he threw a curveball at her, leaving her completely unsure what to expect.

He obviously still distrusted her but they'd managed an entire meal in peace. She supposed she should be grateful for that.

After Wade closed the kitchen door behind himself, Caroline turned back to the table to find Jake standing up as well. "I should go, too. I've got a patient having surgery tomorrow and I promised I'd stop by tonight to answer any of her last-minute questions."

"Really? You do that for all your patients?" She couldn't believe a doctor would go to so much trouble.

"If they need it."

"That's wonderful! It's so refreshing to find a doctor who genuinely cares for his patients as more than just a few dollar signs."

Jake made a face. "When the patient also happens to be my ninth-grade English teacher, I have to be on my best behavior. Agnes Arbuckle was a holy terror. I barely squeaked past her class as it was and I live in dread that if I don't treat her well, she'll give me a pop quiz about gerunds, and when I freeze and botch it she'll find some way to revoke my diploma."

"What's a gerund?" Natalie asked.

"Beats me." Jake winked. "I was never very good at studying."

Caroline laughed. "That was a gerund right there, Natalie. Studying. It's a verb ending in *ing* that acts as noun. Like, *I love dancing.*"

"Really?" Seth stepped into the conversation, though there was a militant light in his eyes. "We ought to go sometime. I can do a mean two-step."

She gave him a look. "Or *I dislike teasing.*"

"I wasn't teasing," he said with a smile, though she thought his heart didn't seem to be in his light flirtation. "Just say the word and I'll show you a night out on the town."

Even with his odd mood, Seth was a remarkably good-looking man. So was Jake, she thought, wondering why on earth she couldn't experience even a little sizzle of the awareness for either of them that surged through her when Wade was in the room.

"Well, hate to break up this grammar lesson but I really do have to run," Jake said. "I'll echo what Wade said. It's been a long time since I've enjoyed a meal like that. Thank you."

Seth slid his chair back. "Yeah, I've got to go, too."

"Where?" Jake asked with a mildly critical look. "The Bandito?"

"What of it?" Seth stalked to the sink, his plate in hand. "Sorry I don't have somewhere more important to go. Like maybe paying house calls to old biddies who only want the attention of a red-blooded young doc like yourself. Or the oh-so-important decision to inseminate the cows by June 1, just like we've been doing at the Cold Creek for fifty years."

The bitterness in his voice shimmered in the air and she saw Jake open his mouth, then apparently think better of whatever he was going to say. He closed it again as Seth headed for the door.

"Thanks for dinner, Caroline," the youngest Dalton brother said, with none of his customary charm, then he slammed the door behind himself.

"Sorry about that." Jake looked annoyed. "Out of all of us, Seth seemed to get most of our father's temper."

She shrugged. "It wasn't aimed at me."

In truth, she felt sorry for him. She wasn't sure why but Wade seemed to discount Seth's ability to help shoulder more of the burden of running the Cold Creek.

None of it was her business, Caroline reminded herself again as she said goodbye to Jake then helped the children through their bath routine—washing hair, finding bath toys, wrapping Tanner's arm and helping him keep it above the water.

As she went through their routine, she thought about the things she had observed that day, of the three motherless children starving for their father's attention.

They each exhibited behaviors she believed were directly linked to Wade's distracted parenting. Natalie had stepped up to mother and boss everyone around; Tanner was a bundle of energy who seemed to find trouble everywhere he went; Cody was clingy, hungry for affection.

And then there was Wade, who buried himself in work, and Seth, who would like to.

Not that she planned to jump to any rushed judgments, Caroline thought wryly.

She had only been here thirty-six hours. She couldn't expect to know and understand all the dynamics of the Dalton family in such a short time. Besides, even if she was spot-on with her assessment, none of it was her business. She was only the temporary help.

After she settled the boys in bed, she crossed the hall to tell Natalie good-night. She found the girl in her bed, her long dark hair still damp and a book propped on her knees.

Nobody walking in this room could ever doubt the girl was horse crazy, Caroline thought with a smile. The walls were covered in horse posters, a knickknack shelf that ran around the entire perimeter of the room about eighteen inches from the ceiling held dozens of horse figures in all colors and sizes, and the bedspread covering those little knees was, of course, equine in design.

"May I come in?" Caroline asked from the doorway.

"Yeah."

She sat on the edge of the bed, drawn to this little girl despite her bossiness. Something about Natalie reminded Caroline of herself, though she wasn't quite sure why.

She had been quiet, almost shy, something that certainly couldn't be said of Natalie. Heaven knows, even if Caroline had shared a similar obsession for anything like Nat's with horses, she and Quinn had never stayed in one place long enough for her to have a collection like this one.

"What are you reading?" she asked.

"Misty of Chincoteague."

"That's a great one."

Natalie shrugged. "It's okay. I've read it three times before."

"Don't you think the very best books are those you can enjoy more every time you read them?"

"I guess."

They lapsed into a not-uncomfortable silence and Caroline wondered what it would be like to have a daughter of her own. It wasn't an unreasonable idea since she had friends with children this age. Still, her mind boggled at the thought.

"The birthday party for your father was very nice. Your hats showed great creativity. I set them aside while I was cleaning up the dishes. I thought maybe we can put them away and save them for whoever's birthday is next in your family."

"That's Grandma," Natalie said. "Her birthday is in November. Mine's not until March."

"We can put them in a box for your grandmother's birthday party, then. She'll love them."

Natalie closed her book, shifting her legs under the comforter.

"My grandma's not coming back, is she?" she said after a moment.

Caroline drew in a sharp breath at the unexpected question. Where did that come from?

And wasn't this the kind of thing Wade should be discussing with his daughter? she thought, irritated at him all over again. If Natalie needed reassurance, she should be able to turn to her father for it, not to a virtual stranger.

But she was here and Wade wasn't, so it looked like she was nominated. "Oh, honey. Of course she's coming back."

The girl's hair rustled as she shook her head. "I heard Uncle Jake and Uncle Seth talking about it. They said how she eloped with your dad. Is it true?"

Caroline squirmed under Natalie's accusing look. She *had* been the one to tell the girl only that Marjorie had gone on a trip with a friend.

"Yes," she finally admitted.

Natalie nodded, her eyes solemn and sad. "So she's not coming back, then."

"Why do you say that?"

"My friend Holly's big sister eloped. She ran away to get married and she never came back. She lives in California and she's gonna have a baby. What if that happens to Grandma?"

Despite the gravity of the conversation, Caroline had to bite back a smile at the idea. "I think I can safely promise you that's not going to happen, honey."

"But what if it does? What if she doesn't come back? Who's gonna take care of me and Tanner and Cody?"

"You still have your dad," she pointed out.

"My dad's too busy with the ranch. He doesn't have time to take me to Girl Scouts or make cookies for my class when it's treat day or fix my hair in the morning. Grandma does all that stuff. If she doesn't come back, who's going to do it?"

"Your grandma's coming back. She said so."

"But what if she doesn't?" Natalie persisted.

"Well, your dad will probably hire somebody to help him."

Natalie didn't look at all thrilled by that idea. "Like a babysitter for all the time?"

"Something like that."

The girl peeked at Caroline under her lashes. "Would you do it if he hired you? You fixed my hair today and the braids looked even better than Grandma's. And your roast beef was the best we ever had, even my dad said so."

"Oh, honey," Caroline said helplessly, not sure how to answer.

"That means no, doesn't it?"

"I can't just stay here. I have a job and a house back in California."

"You could if you wanted to. You just don't want to."

"That's not true. Anyway, you don't have to worry about this, Natalie. Your grandma says she's coming back. Has she ever lied to you before?"

"Yes. She promised she would take me to Girl Scouts today to make scrunchies and she didn't."

Okay, Nat had her there. Caroline sighed. "I know your grandma and I know she loves you very much. She said she's coming back and she will. Whatever happens,

I also know your dad will make sure you have somebody nice to take care of you and your brothers."

She brushed a kiss on Natalie's forehead. "Now go to sleep and stop worrying."

Though she still looked unconvinced, Nat nodded and rolled over, her cheek pressed against yet another horse on her pillow.

Chapter Eight

Wade had been working eighteen-hour days from about the time he'd hit puberty. It was a fact of life on a ranch, something he was used to. When work needed to be done, a man didn't sit around complaining about it, he knuckled down and did it.

If you put off doing what was needed, you only ended up having twice as much to do the next day.

He was used to days when he didn't have five minutes to grab a sandwich, when the minute he finished one task, a dozen more crept up to take its place on his to-do list.

Still, by the time he returned to the ranch house the evening of his birthday dinner, he was more than ready to find his bed. His muscles ached from a hard day of physical labor and his brain was weary from racing around in circles trying to work out the last-minute details before the camera crew arrived on Monday for the pre-interview shots.

He would have loved nothing better than lounging in front of ESPN with a beer and the remote right about now. But since not too many football games were played at eleven on a Thursday night, he figured he would just have to settle for a hot shower and Letterman, while he gave his mind and body time to settle down.

Maybe he could find a piece of birthday cake left, he thought as he parked his pickup at the house and flicked off the headlights. It had been a mighty good cake, even though he'd been too rushed earlier to really savor each bite.

He would have to make sure he remembered to tell Nat she'd done a good job with it, even if Caroline had helped her. As he was pretty sure his daughter would still be in bed before he left in the morning, he'd probably be best to leave her a note about it.

The thought left him feeling vaguely guilty, but he pushed it aside. Another few days and the TV interview would be done. He would still be busy, but at least he wouldn't have that hanging over him, too.

The house was dark except for a small light glowing in the kitchen. It was a silly thing but somehow seeing that glow and knowing Caroline must have left it burning for him warmed him and managed to ease the ache in his muscles just a little.

The night was cool and crisp as he walked into the house, and all was quiet on the Cold Creek.

Wade hung his hat and jacket on the mudroom hook then walked into the kitchen, his mind on cake and, regrettably, on Caroline.

He found both delectable things in the kitchen, the cake on the table and Caroline sitting at the breakfast bar with a laptop open in front of her and papers fanned neatly around her.

She looked up when he walked in, her forehead creased with concentration. Her hair was slipping free from her ponytail and a honey-brown strand lay across the curve of her jawbone, he noticed. She brushed it away, giving him a distracted smile.

In the pale glow from the laptop and the light above the stove, she looked soft and sweet and delicious, and his body instantly jumped with hunger.

"You're still up." It was a stupid thing to say, but for some reason he couldn't seem to hold a coherent thought.

She nodded. "I had some work to catch up on. This seemed a quiet time to do it."

They were alone in the kitchen, the children presumably asleep long ago. "What kind of work?"

"Notes on some of my clients to help me prepare for sessions with them when I return next week."

He almost made a derogatory crack about her work but the words caught in his throat.

He might not see the use in paying somebody else to tell you how to live your life but she was staying in his house, taking care of his kids, and it didn't feel right to give her a hard time about her career.

It was one of those clumsy moments when he couldn't say the first thing that came into his head but couldn't think of anything else to take its place, and they lapsed into an awkward silence.

He was about to excuse himself and head to bed when she finally spoke. "Are you hungry?" she asked.

"There's roast beef left and plenty more cake. I could make you a sandwich if you'd like. With the roast, of course, not the cake."

His mouth watered and dinner seemed a long time ago. On the other hand, he had a funny feeling it wouldn't be exactly the smartest idea he'd ever come up with to fix a snack and sit down to eat it across from Caroline Montgomery, just the two of them in the middle of the night in a warm, cozy kitchen.

Not when he couldn't seem to shake his crazy, unwanted attraction to her.

Since he didn't see any other choice besides grabbing his cake and running away like a coyote-spooked yearling, he opted to pass on the whole thing.

"I'm good. But thanks. You, uh, did a good job with dinner."

"I only made the roast and the potatoes. Natalie did the rest. She worked very hard to give you a memorable birthday dinner."

Did that carefully bland voice hide censure or was it only his guilty conscience?

"Yeah, I was just thinking I should drop her a note about it before I took off in the morning. Tell her what a good job she did and all."

"I suppose you could do that," she said slowly.

"You have a better idea?"

He did his best to keep any trace of defensiveness out of his voice but he wasn't sure he succeeded.

"I just wonder if perhaps it would mean more to her if you could take the time to tell her in person."

A lecture from this woman would be just the thing he needed to cap off a perfect day. He braced himself.

"Maybe, except I'm usually gone before she gets up for school."

"I've noticed." She carefully slid the cap onto her pen and rose from the bar stool. "You're gone before your children awake and not back until long after Natalie and the boys are in bed. I can't help wondering when you do see your children."

Here we go. By force of will, he shoved back the wall of guilt that threatened to crash over him. "I see them."

"When?" she persisted.

"I try to make sure I'm home with them at dinnertime, unless I absolutely can't break away."

"And then you go again."

"Sometimes." Most of the time, he admitted. Not that it was any of Caroline's business. "I also usually have the chance to see the boys for a couple minutes at lunchtime and take them on errands with me when I can."

"Do you think that's all they need from you?" If her voice was at all sarcastic, he would have blown up at her. But she spoke calmly, rationally, and somehow that made it seem worse.

"It's all I have to give them right now. I'm sorry if that doesn't fit your storybook image of what a perfect father ought to be but I'm a little busy here trying to provide for my family."

"You seem to be doing an excellent job of that. Your children don't lack for anything, except maybe your attention."

"Thank you for that two-second analysis, Dr. Montgomery. You'll be the first one I'll turn to if I want an opinion on how to raise my children from a total stranger who has no children of her own and who knows nothing about my situation."

She drew in a sharp breath and her soft, lovely skin seemed to pale a shade.

His guilt kicked up a notch but he shoved it back down. No. This wasn't his fault. She'd asked for it, butting in to things that weren't her concern. If she couldn't take his reaction, she shouldn't have yanked his chain.

He waited for tears or any of those other dirty tricks women used when they were challenged during an argument, but she only nodded. "Fair enough. You're right. I've only been here a day and can't pretend to know all there is know about you and your family. But let me ask you something. What does Natalie want to be when she grows up?"

Another feminine tactic—throw in a non sequitur. What the heck did one thing have to do with the other?

This he had to think about for a minute. "A nurse?" He heard the question in his voice and quickly repeated it with more confidence. "She wants to be a nurse."

"Maybe. But what she most wants to be at this moment is a barrel racer, like her mother."

Really? He hadn't even realized Nat knew of Andi's high-school rodeo days.

Before he could answer, Caroline went on. "What's her favorite color? What friend asked her to sleep over tomorrow night? What grade did she get on her math test, the one that was the highest in her class?"

He glared at her, angry at himself for not knowing the answers to her interrogation and angry with her for pushing him on this when it was none of her damn business.

Though it strained his self-control to the limit, he managed to contain his temper.

He wasn't about to engage in a shouting match with Caroline Montgomery in his own kitchen. No good could possibly come of it. And besides, there was a very real chance he would lose, since everything she'd said was right on the money.

"I don't know," he finally said quietly. "I'm sure it just makes your day to hear me admit that. I don't know those things about my daughter. I guess that makes me the world's worst father."

To his considerable dismay, she reached out and touched his arm, and he felt the heat of it through every nerve ending. "Of course it doesn't make you a bad father. I never meant to imply such a thing. You're busy. It must be hard work running a ranch of this size. I understand that."

To his relief, she withdrew her hand and frowned. "But I'm not so sure your children do."

"They will. My brothers and I figured it out."

He didn't add that he and his brothers hadn't much minded their father being consumed by the ranch all the time as long as it had kept the son of a bitch away from them.

He couldn't be a completely lousy father—how could he be, since he wasn't anything like Hank Dalton? He was never cruel to his children; he didn't taunt them, or berate them or make them feel lower than the lowliest vermin on the ranch.

"Did you?" Her voice was soft but it still cut through his memories like a buzz saw.

"Did I what?"

"Understand about your father?"

His glare sliced at her. "What's that supposed to mean?"

She shouldn't have said anything. This wasn't at all what she'd wanted to talk to him about tonight. She was concerned only for his children, only Nat and the boys.

Still, in the day and a half she'd been on the ranch, she had begun to wonder if anyone at the Cold Creek was truly happy. Wade certainly didn't seem to be, and this evening at dinner she had witnessed firsthand Seth's unhappiness.

She couldn't put her finger on why she thought this, but there was a kind of sadness to the ranch, a deep and profound melancholy that seemed to permeate the air.

She'd thought it was because he and his children were still grieving for the wife and mother they had lost, but now she wondered if it went deeper than that.

For a moment there after he'd mentioned his father, she had seen something in Wade's eyes, an old pain that suddenly made him seem big and lost and lonely, and that tore at her heart.

"Nothing," she murmured. "I'm sorry. None of my business."

He leaned forward suddenly and was once more the hard man she'd come to know.

"No, you started this. You might as well finish it. What did you mean by that snide little 'did you'?"

She hadn't meant it to sound snide. Obviously his father was a sore subject and she chose her words carefully.

"Marjorie told me something of your father's personality during our coaching sessions. Not much, but enough that I know he wasn't an easy man to live with."

"That's one word for it. My father was a stone-cold bastard, there's no secret about that. He figured he owned everything and everyone on the Cold Creek. We all had to walk his line or else. I used to think he invented that old phrase about my way or the highway. He sure liked to use it enough."

He shook himself a little. "But I'm not my father. I would never be deliberately cruel to my kids."

"Not deliberately, no. But they notice your absence in their lives far more than you might think. When parents are too distant and distracted, no matter what the reason, children can't help but view it as a rejection. They begin to wonder what makes them so unlovable and find themselves doing all kinds of crazy things to find that attention they need."

Like cutting off all her hair when she was twelve or getting her nose pierced the year she'd turned fourteen, all in the hopes that Quinn might look at *her* once, instead of the next deal.

Somehow Wade must have picked up on her thoughts.

"That sounds like the voice of experience." He moved forward slightly, his eyes an intense blue in the low lighting.

She forced herself not to flinch. "We're not talking about me," she said coolly, wondering how this conversation had suddenly twisted around to her.

"Maybe we should be."

"My childhood isn't very interesting and has no bearing on this discussion," she said, then mentally cringed at the cool, prim note she heard in her voice.

"I think it does. What kind of a father was Quinn Montgomery? The doting kind who adored your every move and let you get away with murder? Or the stern, authoritarian type who laid down the law and insisted you follow it?"

Neither. Quinn had been just like Wade. Distracted, distant. Disinterested. Maybe that's why it was so painful for her to watch. Her father loved her, but on his own schedule, when he could fit her in between scams. Not when she needed him most.

She certainly wasn't going to share that with Wade, though.

"I'm sorry," she said, gathering up her notes and closing up her computer. "I shouldn't have said anything. It's been a long day and we're both tired. I'll see you in the morning."

"Running away?"

Her gaze flashed to his and she wasn't sure how to read the expression there.

"No. I just..."

"You should be. It would be better for both of us."

Before she could figure out that odd statement, he stepped forward, his eyes dark and stormy, and an instant later his mouth descended to hers.

For one shocked second, she froze as his powerful arms captured her and tugged her against his unyielding strength, as his mouth moved slowly over hers.

He tasted dusty and male, a combination she somehow found irresistible, and she softened in his arms, giving in to the attraction that had been buzzing through her like an insistent hummingbird from the moment she'd arrived at the Cold Creek.

She shivered as every cell surged to awareness, to a sweet and heavy arousal, and she was lost to everything but this—the taste and scent and feel of him surrounding her with heat and strength.

What had brought them to this? She wasn't quite sure. One moment they'd been arguing, the next here they were, mouths tangled together, both breathing hard as they tasted and touched and explored.

He didn't like her and thought she was a nosy busybody. So why was he holding her with a kind of desperation, one hand buried in her hair, the other at the small of her back drawing her close enough she could feel the hard jut of his arousal?

She was vaguely aware of the world outside their embrace, of the pig-shaped clock ticking above the stove and a sudden breeze rattling the glass panes and the hard countertop of the breakfast bar digging into her back as he pressed her against it.

But none of it mattered.

Her entire world had condensed to this moment, to this man with his solid strength and the sadness in his eyes.

"You smell so good." The low whisper in her ear was more arousing even than his touch. "Like homemade vanilla ice cream fresh from my grandma's old tin ice-cream maker."

She shivered as his mouth slowly slid down her jawline then found the rapid pulse in her neck.

He kissed her there, then his mouth found hers again and Caroline decided she could cheerfully die right here in the Cold Creek kitchen as long as Wade Dalton could kiss her to heaven.

One of her clients had reached a goal earlier in the year of parachuting out of an airplane for her fiftieth birthday. She'd described a freefall to Caroline as incredible, not so much a sensation of falling as flying, soaring above the earth with arms outstretched and the wind rushing to meet you.

For the first time, here in Wade's arms with his mouth hard on hers, Caroline began to understand what she'd meant by that and she never wanted this twirling, whirling freefall to stop.

One of his hands moved to her waist and slid beneath her shirt just enough to touch the bare skin above the waistband of her jeans. She moaned, her arms tight around his neck, and leaned into his slow, arousing touch, desperate for more.

She wasn't sure what sound intruded first, the scrape of a boot on the steps outside the kitchen door or the low, tuneless whistling—she only knew someone else was coming.

No. Go away, she thought, but the sounds drew nearer. She didn't know how, but at the last moment she managed to organize her scattered brain cells just enough to yank out of Wade's arms half a second before the door opened with a squeak.

Seth stood in the doorway, a basket of laundry in his arms and those heartbreakingly blue eyes wide with surprise. His gaze shifted from her to Wade and then back again, and she knew hot color was soaking her cheeks. Beside her, she could hear Wade's ragged breathing and she was mortified to see the surprise in Seth's eyes give way to speculation.

"I didn't think anybody else would be up. Sorry to interrupt."

"You didn't," Caroline said quickly, compelled for

some insane reason to protect Wade from his brother's knowing look. "We were, um, talking about the children."

Not exactly a lie, she told herself. They *had* been talking about the children right before that earthshaking kiss.

"Right. Must have been a pretty heated conversation. You're both looking a little flush. What were you doing, comparing your philosophies about corporal punishment? That's bound to get anybody a little hot. Personally—and I hope this doesn't make me sound like a cretin—I come down on the side that sometimes a little swat on the behind is the only thing you can do to get the little buggers' attention. You can give all the timeouts in the world but they won't be as effective as one well-timed hand to the tush. Don't you agree, Wade?"

"Whatever," Wade snapped, looking so completely stunned by what had just happened that Caroline wanted to die of mortification.

"Well, I was only going to throw in a load of laundry," Seth said. "But I can certainly come back later if you're not done, uh, talking."

"Leave it alone," Wade growled to his brother.

To her immense gratification, Seth held his tongue, though he did nothing to hide his amusement.

Caroline decided she had no option left but to flee. "Do your laundry," she said to Seth. "I was just heading to bed. Good night."

The last was directed to both of them but she hurried from the kitchen without daring to look at Wade.

She might never be able to look at him again, not after the way she had responded instantly in his arms as if he'd set spark to dry tinder.

Chapter Nine

Wade watched Caroline rush from the kitchen and wondered if he would ever be able to taste vanilla ice cream again without remembering those incredible few moments she had burned in his arms.

"You're an idiot," he growled, though he wasn't completely sure whether his words were aimed at his brother or himself.

"That's the rumor." Seth grinned, unoffended, and headed for the laundry room just off the kitchen.

"I *am* sorry I interrupted," he called over his shoulder. "I should have knocked first. I just never expected to find my cold and passionless older brother locking lips with our beautiful new stepsister."

"She's *not* our stepsister, damn it!"

This seemed to amuse Seth even more. Grinning like a fool, he started the wash cycle.

Wade thought about going upstairs for that shower he so desperately needed—the one that would now by necessity have to be frigid—then decided he might as well settle at least one of his hungers.

He was cutting a slice of leftover birthday cake when Seth wandered back in.

"Oooh, cake. Mind sharing a piece of that?"

He would have preferred for Seth to take that amused, knowing look and cram it. But it was hard to smirk and eat at the same time, so he gestured to the cake server with his fork. "Help yourself."

"Thanks. I worked up one hell of an appetite down at the Bandito tonight. Bunch of women from New York are staying out at the Swan Valley Dude Ranch, sort of a girls' week out, I guess. They were in the mood for a little cowboy boogie, if you know what I mean. I couldn't let them go home disappointed."

Sometimes he wondered if Seth had been born knowing how to irritate him or if he'd honed the skill through years of study and practice. His brother knew how much he disliked hearing about his exploits so, of course, he delighted in sharing at every opportunity.

He was damn sure not in the mood tonight to hear them, so he decided to change the subject.

"Do you think I'm a poor father?"

Seth froze, the fork halfway to his mouth, then he set it down like it was handblown china. "Is that what Caroline says?"

"Not in so many words."

Seth cocked his head, his eyes baffled but moderately impressed. "Okay so explain to me how a woman goes from questioning your parenting skills to swapping saliva with you?"

To his dismay, Wade could feel his ears turn red. "We were just talking," he mumbled.

"Right. That's why when I came in, her sweet little mouth was all swollen and her cheeks matched the pink of Mom's climbing roses. All that talking, huh?"

Served him right for thinking he could ever have a serious conversation with Seth. "Just drop it. Forget I said anything."

"No, you want to know if I think you're a poor father." To Wade's surprise, his brother didn't offer any more wisecracks and he even appeared to give the matter some thought. "I don't think I've ever heard you say a harsh word to Nat and the boys, unlike our own dear old dad."

"That has to count for something."

"Something," Seth agreed, taking another bite of cake. "You're not half the bastard he was."

"Gee, thanks."

"On the other hand, you do tend to leave a lot of the work to Mom, when it comes to the kids."

First Caroline now Seth. He sighed. "What else am I supposed to do? Can somebody just tell me that? I don't have much choice. The ranch won't run itself."

Seth's too-handsome features seemed to harden a little and for a moment Wade almost thought he saw bitterness flicker in his eyes. "No, it won't. But your kids won't raise themselves, either. What if Mom decides not to come back?"

"Don't think that hasn't been keeping me up at night." And now he would have memories of kissing

Caroline to help do the job. "I don't know. I guess I'll have to figure something out. Hire a housekeeper or something."

"Or a ranch manager."

"Can't say I'm crazy about either one of those ideas." He sighed again and took a sip of water. "This wasn't the way things were supposed to turn out. This whole single-father thing sucks."

"Imagine your life without the kids, though," Seth pointed out.

For one brief second, Wade considered how much less stress he would have in his life right now.

Yeah, his life might be less frenzied. But it would also be bleak and miserable.

No Natalie, with her rapid chatter and her freely offered opinions, no Tanner and all that energy, no Cody to cuddle up with him on Sunday afternoons while they napped and watched fishing shows. It didn't even bear thinking about.

He loved his children but it was still tough raising them on his own, wondering if every move he made was the wrong one.

Caroline didn't help things, coming here, stirring him up, making him question himself even more.

"So while you and Caroline were, uh, talking, did she offer any advice for you?"

Not at the time, but he was willing to bet she had a few choice suggestions for him after that kiss. A few of them might even have something to do with the kids.

"I'm sure she's working up to that," he murmured. "I imagine before she goes back to California, I'll have an earful of advice. The woman's not exactly shy about expressing her opinions."

He wanted her gone, he told himself.

So why did his chest feel hollow just at the thought of it?

How could she ever face him again?

The sun hadn't yet managed its rigorous daily climb above the Tetons but Caroline was already dressed. She wasn't quite ready for the day, though, as she curled up in the window seat of her bedroom, a blanket across her knees, gazing out at the quiet, dark ranch.

Her eyes burned, gritty and tired, and she wondered if she had managed any sleep at all. Her mind couldn't seem to stop racing around and around that stunning kiss.

It was just a kiss, she reminded herself. Nothing to get so worked up about.

But that wild conflagration certainly seemed on a completely different level from your regular, everyday kiss. One moment they had been arguing about the children, the next they'd been tangled together, wild and hungry. If Seth hadn't wandered into the kitchen, she could only imagine how far they might have taken things.

Unless Wade was a better actor than she, both of them had been lost to the world, to propriety, to the sheer *insanity* of the sudden shocking heat between them.

Where had it come from? What strange command did he have over her? She had scarcely recognized herself in that needy, hungry creature in his arms the night before.

She was thirty years old, far from a giddy teenager, and though her love life wasn't exactly the stuff of legend, she'd enjoyed a few relationships she considered serious.

Each of them had been pleasant in its own way. Yes, that was exactly the word. *Pleasant.* Calm, comfortable, easy.

The heat she and Wade generated had been something else entirely, something completely out of her experience.

It had been raw and fierce and wild, almost frightening in its intensity. She had never had any idea she could burn like that and she wasn't sure she liked it.

Perhaps because of her chaotic childhood, she preferred the comfort of order and calm in her relationships. What she'd experienced in Wade's arms the night before had been anything *but* ordered and calm.

She supposed her reaction disturbed her most because she didn't understand it. Wade was so different from the usual sort of man she dated. He was powerful, forceful, the kind of man who seemed to consume all the oxygen molecules in every room he entered. Despite that, there was also a deep loneliness about him that drew her like a magnet.

She was a sucker for anyone in need, always had been. She wanted to comfort and heal, to hold him close and absorb his pain.

What must he think of her for responding so passionately to him? She cringed just thinking about it.

He already seemed to think she had ulterior motives for coming to the ranch, that she and Quinn were part of some complex scheme to drain the Cold Creek coffers. What if he thought her response to him was another indication that she had somehow set her sights on him as part of their twisted plans?

Nothing could be further from the truth.

Yes, she was attracted to him. But that heated kiss in the kitchen was the only thing they could ever share, even if Wade was interested in more. She had coached enough people struggling through bad relationships to know that one based only on attraction would never survive. And though she'd only known the man a few days, what she had seen didn't lead her to believe he was a good fit for her, relationship-wise.

She could never let herself care for a man who ranked his own children so low on his priority list. She had lived through it herself and knew the pain firsthand.

So how did she make it through the next few days? she wondered as she yawned and stood up. She couldn't avoid the man—it was his house, after all. In a few moments, she would probably see him over breakfast, when she would have to smile and be polite and pretend nonchalance about their scalding embrace.

Though she wanted just the opposite for his children, for her own sake, she had to hope he would be even more busy the next few days as the television interview approached. With any luck, he would be too distracted by that to pay much attention to her.

And while he was busy ignoring her, she would work on shaking free of her unwanted attraction toward the man.

How hard could it be?

Her resolve to keep her distance lasted all of an hour—and then she saw him again.

She had to admit, she had been relieved not to find him in the kitchen when she finally made her way there, though Seth showed up a few moments after she started frying bacon and mixing pancake batter. She assumed Wade had already left for the morning, as someone had made a fresh pot of coffee on the coffeemaker and left a dirty cup in the sink.

The most she had to contend with before the children came down was Seth's flirtation, though it seemed more mechanical than sincere. She didn't know the youngest Dalton brother well but this was the first time she'd seen him so pensive.

The compliments he gave her were almost benign, with none of his flowery prose. He also didn't make any cracks about the scene he had to know he'd interrupted the night before.

She almost asked if he was feeling well but decided that would seem presumptuous.

The children woke soon after Seth had left with a subdued thank you for breakfast. After that, she didn't have time to worry about either Dalton brother, she was too busy taking care of the next generation.

For the next hour she ran nonstop—helping Nat find her library books, rewrapping the bandage on Tanner's burn that had slipped loose in the night, and changing and dressing Cody, who for some reason decided to cling to her like an orangutan baby while she fixed plates of pancakes and bacon for the children.

She was on the floor mopping up the second spilled orange juice of the morning due to Tanner's awkward use of his bandaged hand when she heard the door creak behind her.

Some instinct told her who had come in and she froze, mortified at being caught on her hands and knees, her rear end in the air and Cody leaning against her hip.

Grabbing Cody to keep him upright as she shifted position, she rose quickly to her feet and faced Wade.

Why did the air seem high and thin suddenly? She couldn't seem to breathe, her mind jumping with images of the last time she had faced him here in this kitchen.

"Morning."

Wade's deep-voiced greeting encompassed the room and his progeny. He took off his hat as he walked inside but, instead of hanging it up on the customary hook, he kept it in his hands. She assumed that indicated he didn't plan to stay long.

"Hey Dad, guess what?" Tanner started in with his favorite phrase. "Caroline put a new bandage on my hand and she had to wrap it three times because I was moving too much and she said it was grosser than a whole room full of stinky socks."

"I hope you told her thanks for helping you," he said gruffly. "Not everybody would be willing to face something grosser than a room full of stinky socks first thing in the morning."

"I did."

"Good."

After an awkward pause, he shifted his hat to his other hand and finally met Caroline's gaze.

Her insides twirled and she could swear the temperature of the room had just kicked up at least ten degrees.

"Did I already miss Nat's bus?" Though he directed the question to her, he didn't maintain eye contact and she had to wonder if this encounter was as awkward for him as she was finding it.

"No. She just ran upstairs to change her shirt. Tanner spilled orange juice on the one she was wearing."

"Oh."

She was staring at his mouth, she realized, remembering in vivid detail how it had moved over hers the night before, licking and tasting and exploring....

She quickly jerked her gaze away, horrified at herself as heat soaked her cheeks.

"Um, would you like some breakfast?"

"I grabbed some bread and jam with my coffee this morning before I headed out. I don't have much time, just a few minutes, really."

Big surprise there, she thought, but before she could say anything, Nat burst back into the kitchen.

She stopped when she saw her father. "Hi, Dad! I thought you guys were bringing down the range cows from Hightop today."

"We are. We're leaving in a minute."

He rubbed the back of his neck. "I, uh, just wanted to catch you before you left for school. I didn't have a chance to talk to you much last night but I wanted you to know the birthday cake you made was great. I had another piece last night before I went to bed and so did Uncle Seth. We both said as how the second piece was even better than the first. I just wanted you to know."

He said all this without looking at Caroline and she had to admit, she was grateful. She couldn't have said anything past the lump in her throat, stunned that he took her advice about speaking to Natalie in person.

She'd forgotten that part of their conversation because of what had come after, but obviously Wade hadn't. Here he was first thing in the morning, his hat in his hands, taking time away from his busy schedule to give his daughter some of the attention she craved from him.

Caroline could swear she heard the bump and clatter of her heart tumbling to his feet at the look Wade's simple words had put on Natalie's face. The girl's smile couldn't have stretched any wider and she looked like she was ready to take flight.

"You're welcome."

Backpack forgotten, Nat ran to her father, throwing her arms around his waist. Wade returned her hug, then waited patiently while she grabbed up her jacket and her school things, talking a mile a minute.

"It wasn't hard to make," she gushed. "I just followed the recipe like Grandma showed me and Caroline helped me crack the eggs and put on the frosting. I knew you would like it. I *knew* it. Grandma says your sweet tooth is just as bad now as it was when you were Tanner's age. She said you could finish off a cake all by yourself if you put your mind to it."

"Between Seth and me, we did a pretty good job with yours," he said, though he didn't look thrilled at either his daughter or his mother for sharing that information.

"Do you want me to make you another one today? I can. I can make one anytime you want. I think I can even do the eggs by myself next time."

"Thanks, honey. I think one is enough for now but I'll let you know when I'm ready for more."

"You'd better go or you're going to miss the bus," Caroline murmured, though she was loathe to interrupt the girl's excitement.

Natalie hurried toward the door, where she paused and turned back, still glowing. "Dad, when I come home from school can I help you unload the cows? I won't get in the way, I promise. I just want to watch the hazing."

He opened his mouth and Caroline could see the refusal forming in his expression, but he surprised her by nodding after a moment. "If we're still at it, you can come down to the pens."

Natalie gave a delighted shout, then rushed out the door toward the bus stop.

"Can I help, too, Dad?" Tanner jumped down from his chair. "Hey, can I come up to the mountains with you to bring 'em down, too? I won't get in the way either."

Caroline couldn't contain a smile at that bald-faced lie. She was learning Tanner's best skill was getting in the way.

She stepped in so Wade wouldn't have to be the one to say no. "I need your help around here. We're going to run into town and do some grocery shopping."

"Shopping's stupid. I want to help with the roundup."

"Next time, partner," Wade spoke firmly. "When your arm's all better, okay?"

"Why does Nat get to watch?"

"Because she's older—and because she doesn't have a bum hand she needs to keep clean."

"You said bum, Dad!" Tanner chortled.

"Right. And I'll smack yours if I catch you down at the pens today, you hear me? Those range cows are quick and mean. You stay clear."

Tanner pouted. "I know. I'm not a baby like Cody."

"Then you're old enough and smart enough to obey me, right?"

"I guess." Tanner looked disappointed but didn't push it as he turned back to his breakfast.

Wade stood there another second then shoved his hat back on. "I've got to run. The crew is waiting for me."

This time he met Caroline's gaze directly and she

could swear she saw something fierce and hot leap into those blue eyes before he shielded them again. "I meant what I said to Tanner. We'll be bringing two hundred head down today in a couple of batches. Best if you keep the boys clear of them. They can be vicious."

"I will," she promised.

Wade turned to go but she stopped him with a hand to his arm. Heat sparked between them and she quickly dropped her fingers. "Sorry. I just…I wanted to tell you I was touched by what you just did for Nat."

He looked more than a little embarrassed. "It wasn't anything."

"Don't say that. It might have been a little thing but surely you could see it meant the world to her."

He opened his mouth to say something then seemed to change his mind. "I've got to run," he said abruptly, then hurried out of the kitchen without another word.

Chapter Ten

The lovebirds finally called to check in just as Wade was following the last semitrailer full of range cows back to the ranch later that day.

He almost didn't pick up his cell phone when it rang, distracted by all he still had to do that day, and it took a moment for his mother's voice to register.

He barely recognized it. She sounded about a dozen years younger.

"Where the he—heck are you?" he asked.

"Reno, honey. Didn't you get my note?"

"Yeah, I got it. I just still can't believe you'd run off like that."

"I'm sorry, honey, but we just couldn't wait another day to be together. You understand, don't you?"

Not in the slightest, but he decided saying so would be mean so he kept his mouth shut.

"Are you coming back?" he asked instead.

"I told you I was, didn't I? Actually that's what I'm calling about. We were planning to be back Monday or Tuesday but now we're talking about driving over to the coast. We thought we'd spend a few days packing up Quinn's place in San Francisco and then drive down to see his daughter in Santa Cruz. Will you and the kids be all right for a few more days if we do that?"

Mentally, he was pounding his head against the steering wheel a couple dozen times. In reality, he just grimaced. "We'll survive. But you won't find Montgomery's daughter in California."

"Sure we will. That's where she lives."

"Not at the present. She's here."

"Who's there?"

"Caroline. She showed up the morning after you left."

"Caroline Montgomery?"

"That's what I said, isn't it?"

"Why, that was two days ago. She's still there?"

Only two days? It felt like forever. He sighed. "Yeah. She offered to stay and help with the kids."

"And you let her?"

The shock in her voice made him defensive. "You picked a hell of a time to run off, Mom. The crew from the network is showing up in three days and things here are a mess. I didn't know what else to do."

He heard silence on the line, then Marjorie's muffled voice telling someone—her huggy bear, he assumed—about Caroline. A moment later, his mother returned to the line.

"It's just like her to see you needed help and settle right in to do what she can. Isn't she wonderful?"

He was still reserving judgment on that one. "She's something, all right," he muttered.

"I just *knew* you'd like her once you met her. I'm sure Nat and the boys adore her already."

Too much. They were going to miss her when she left. "You didn't give me too many choices," he repeated.

"I'm losing the signal here, honey. I didn't quite catch that."

"You left things in a mess here, Mom," he said loudly. "What kind of example do you think that sets to the kids when they see their grandmother run off with some guy she never even met in person?"

"Sorry I can't hear you. These darn cell phones. Works fine one minute, then you feel like you're talking to yourself the next."

Marjorie still sounded giddy and he had to wonder if she really couldn't hear him or if she was faking because she didn't want to listen to any of his lectures.

"Hope you can still hear me because all I'm getting on my end is static," she went on. "Since you've got Caroline there, I know the kids are in good hands. I guess that means we can go to San Francisco without worrying. We'll be back by Wednesday. Thursday at the latest. Tell the kids I love them and I'll see them soon."

Before he realized it, she had severed the connection. He tossed the phone on the passenger seat, though what he really wanted was to chuck the damn thing through the windshield.

Somebody suddenly rapped on his window and he turned to find Seth on the other side. He rolled down the window.

"What's the holdup?" Seth asked.

Wade winced when he realized the crew was all lined up behind him waiting to get through and unload the cattle.

"I love that woman but sometimes, I swear she makes me absolutely crazy."

Seth looked confused. "What woman?"

"Mom. That was her on the phone. Apparently she and her Romeo are having such a wonderful time on their honeymoon they've decided to extend it."

Seth winced. "I don't even want to go there, man. It's an image I don't need in my head."

"They're not ready to come back by Sunday since they want to drive to the coast. Now it's looking like they won't be back until Wednesday or Thursday, which leaves us stuck with Caroline for a few more days, if she's up for it."

"No real hardship there. You don't often find a woman who is sweet as sugar, can cook like that and who looks great while she's doing it. I like her."

"You like anything that doesn't have a Y chromosome."

Seth grinned. "True enough. But I especially like Caroline. You have to admit, she has plenty of grit to pitch right in like she did. Most women would have taken off running the first time they caught sight of your little Dalton gang."

She did seem to be good for the kids. All three of them had taken to her immediately.

He thought of the way he'd seen her that morning when he'd walked into the kitchen, with Cody leaning on her while she worked, like the boy didn't want to let her get two feet away.

"I like having her here," Seth said again, then he grinned. "And judging by that scene in the kitchen I so rudely interrupted last night, I can't help but think you do, too."

Yeah, that was the whole problem and the reason he wanted her gone as soon as possible.

He did like her, entirely too much. He hadn't stopped thinking about her all day. Of her mouth, soft and warm and welcoming, of the soft, sexy sounds she'd made when he'd kissed her, of her small hands buried in his hair, sending shivers of pleasure down his spine.

He shifted in the seat, furious at himself for going down that road again. The night before had been a colossal mistake, one he would make sure never happened again.

"I would like having Mom back where she belongs a hell of a lot more," he muttered, then threw the truck in gear and drove through the gate, leaving his brother watching after him.

Caroline had to admit that even after five years of coaching people to break old patterns and alter old habits—years when she had seen some of her clients make remarkable changes—she found it amazing how quickly she adapted to a new way of life.

Four days after that stunning kiss, she stood at the kitchen window washing lunch dishes and looking out at a clear, beautiful October day. The trees outside the window were ablaze with color and leaves fluttered down on the breeze.

Beyond them, the jagged, snow-capped Tetons provided their magnificent backdrop to the scene and she thought how lucky the Daltons were to enjoy that view every day.

She had been at the ranch for six days and her life in Santa Cruz seemed far away.

She never would have expected to find such contentment here. The children had already wiggled their way into her heart and she found each day with them a delight.

Over the weekend, she'd found Nat to have a funny sense of humor, a sweet girl who mothered her little brothers and who missed her own mother. Tanner was so bright and so inquisitive, he had a million questions about everything. And she adored Cody for his sweet disposition and eagerness to love.

She would miss them all when she returned to California, even Seth with his teasing flirtations and the three quiet, polite ranch hands she had met briefly.

And Wade. Would she miss Wade?

She sighed as she dried the last dish and returned it to the cupboard. Most definitely.

She already did, as she hadn't seen him for more than a few minutes at a time since that night in the kitchen.

With his impeccable timing, Tanner wandered into the kitchen just as she finished. "We're bored. There's nothing to do."

That was the biggest challenge with this one. His attention span was painfully short and keeping him entertained and occupied had been a great challenge, especially with his burned hand and the precautions they had to take because of it.

"Can we go play in the sandbox?" he asked now, his big blue eyes wearing a pleading expression that was tough to resist.

She stiffened her spine and shook her head. "Honey, you know you can't until your bandage comes off. But you only have to wait one more day, remember? That's not so bad. Your uncle Jake said everything's looking good with your burn and you won't have to have the mummy claw of death much longer."

Tanner made his trademark menacing lunge at her and she played along, shrieking and backing away as he advanced. When she couldn't go backward any more, she caught him in a quick hug, which he returned with a willingness that warmed her heart.

"You can hang on one more day, can't you?"

"I don't want to," he complained. "Why can't you just take it off now so I can go outside and play? You take it off to change it."

"Because then your uncle would be mad at me."

Tanner's expression turned crafty. "He won't spank you, though, 'cause you're a girl and my dad says boys don't hit girls."

She laughed. "Nice try. But even with that threat out of the way, I'm not going to take off your bandage, kiddo. I'm under orders."

His sigh was heavy and put-upon, and she hid a smile as she reached for Cody to keep him from dumping the garbage can.

"Care, Care," the toddler chanted, throwing his arms tightly around her neck.

"Why don't we find jackets and your hats and we'll go outside for a walk?"

"Can we go see Sunshine?" Tanner asked.

"Of course. But we have to stay out of your dad's way, right?"

Tanner nodded. "Yeah, 'cause the TV people are here."

"That's right. And this is important to your father."

The actual interview wasn't until the next day, but the network had sent an advance crew to lay the groundwork for it and to shoot visuals around the ranch of Wade and his crew working.

It was a beautiful day for a walk and for a video shoot, Caroline thought as she followed the two little bobbing cowboy hats outside. The sky was almost painfully blue, with only a few high clouds. It was cool, though, and she was grateful for her sweater.

On their way to the barn and Tanner's pony, they crunched through leaves and tried to catch them in the air as they fluttered down under the spreading branches of the big maples along the fence.

Maybe she ought to ask Wade where to find some rakes and she and the boys could spend the afternoon making piles and jumping in them.

Cody's pony nickered when he saw them and came trotting over for a treat.

"Please can I ride him, Care-line? Please? I'll forget how if I don't."

She debated it. His hand was much improved and, if he wore a glove, she didn't see the harm in allowing it. "Maybe when Nat gets home to help you saddle him, okay?"

"Yes!" Tanner made a triumphant fist in the air just as she heard adult voices.

She turned to find Wade walking around the barn with three others, two men carrying camera equipment and a young woman in jeans and new-looking boots with a clipboard and a cell phone.

She pondered how best to sneak out of their way before Wade and his companions spotted them. Before she could, though, the boys caught sight of their father.

"Daddy, Daddy!" Cody wriggled out of her hold like a budding Houdini and raced to his father, Tanner right on his heels.

Caroline hurried after them, arriving just in time to watch Cody hold his arms out for his father to lift him up.

"Sorry," she said a little breathlessly. "They're faster than me."

Wade's features looked annoyed but he didn't say anything, only gave in to Cody's demands and picked him up.

She had to admit, they made a charming picture—the sexy cowboy and his two very cute little buckaroos in their matching cowboy hats.

Apparently, she wasn't the only one who thought so. The woman with the clipboard seemed to melt into a gushy pile right there next to the horse pasture.

"Oh my gosh, they are *so* precious. We have to include them in the shoot."

Wade blinked. "The boys?"

"Absolutely!" The woman was young and attractive and had a look in her eye that reminded Caroline of some of her clients who became so totally one-dimensional they weren't able to focus on anything but work.

If she were one of her clients, Caroline would probably tell this young woman to quickly find a hobby outside work before she burned herself up like Caroline had done at social work.

"Just thinking out loud here," the woman went on, "but maybe we could do something along the lines of building a legacy for your children's future or something, as those who make their living from the land have been doing for generations. I'll have to run it past the reporter."

She turned to Caroline suddenly, her features friendly. "I'm sorry. I'm Darci Perez, Mrs. Dalton. I'm producing the story about your husband and the Cold Creek."

Caroline froze, unexpected heat flashing through her at the idea. Her gaze collided with Wade's and she found the aghast expression on his face the height of humiliation.

"He's not my husband," Caroline said quickly—too quickly, she realized, when the producer looked surprised at her vehemence.

The woman winced. "Sorry. I should know better than to jump to conclusions like that."

"Tanner, don't touch anything," Wade broke in sharply and Caroline saw that one of the cameramen had set his equipment on a bale of hay and Tanner, of course, had homed in on it like a bee on a honeysuckle bush.

Tanner froze and Wade turned back to the conversation. "I'm a widower," he told the producer. A muscle flexed in his jaw, as if just saying the word was difficult.

Darci Perez looked even more uncomfortable. "That's probably in the background information I have about you. I should have read it more closely. I'm so sorry."

"Don't worry about it," Wade said, then glared again at Tanner, who, despite his father's warning, had sidled closer to the equipment. "What did I tell you about not touching anything?"

If Caroline hadn't survived six days with the boy, she might have been taken in by his angelic expression. "I'm just looking, Daddy. With my eyes, not my hand or my mummy claw of death."

"Keep it that way, bud."

The producer was studying her expectantly so Caroline stepped forward, her hand outstretched. "I'm Caroline Montgomery, a friend of the family. I'm staying here for a few days to help Wade with the children while his mother is out of town."

The woman shook her hand. "That name is familiar. Have we met?"

"I don't believe so."

Darci frowned and then her expression brightened. "I know! Didn't you write an article for *Glamour* a few months ago about top ten best ways to guarantee yourself a happy, fulfilling life?"

Caroline was flattered, she had to admit. "I did. I'm shocked you remembered the byline. Most people skip right over them."

"Only because I practically have the thing memorized." The woman grinned. "I've done the exact opposite of at least half of the things on your list but I'm working on it."

Caroline smiled. "Progress is good."

"Don't you think you should be going back to the house now?" Wade asked and she saw that it was all he could do to hold onto Cody, who'd decided he wanted down now and was wriggling for all he was worth.

Darci observed the boy's struggles with interest. "He looks like a handful. That must be an interesting challenge, a single father trying to raise his young children and run a ranch of this size as well."

"*Interesting* is one word for it," Wade said.

"I'll mention that to the reporter, too. He might want to follow up on that angle."

Wade would absolutely detest discussing his personal life on camera, Caroline knew. She wondered how to help him avoid it, then remembered it was none of her business.

"Come on, boys. Let's go," she said. She took Cody from Wade and turned around for Tanner, then drew in a quick breath when she found him trying to heft the large camera off the hay bale.

"Tanner! Put that down!" Wade barked. The boy jumped at his tone and hurried to obey but the camera slid out of his bandaged hand and landed in the dirt with a heavy, sickening thud.

"Tanner! I told you not to touch anything." Wade's features looked harsh and angry. "Now look what you've done!"

Tanner's lip trembled. "I'm sorry, Daddy. I didn't mean to. It slipped out of my hand."

"You shouldn't have been messing with it in the first place. When are you ever going to learn to listen to me?"

Tanner gazed around at the circle of adults looking down at him, then at his father's glower. He let out a little distressed cry then took off running around the side of the barn.

Wade stared after him like he wasn't quite sure what to do. Exasperated, Caroline handed Cody back to him and started out after the boy.

Chapter Eleven

Caroline followed the upset boy around the corner of the barn, wondering how on earth his little legs could move so fast.

She assumed he was heading for the house but then he seemed to catch sight of something distracting. Suddenly, in mid-stride he switched directions and headed toward the pens to the east of the barn.

Caroline stopped dead, her blood suddenly coated in a thin, crackly layer of ice, when she saw what was inside the corral. At least a dozen range cows and their calves munched hay, their wickedly sharp horns gleaming in the afternoon sun.

She remembered Wade's warning about the range cows and what she'd learned in the few days she'd been on the Cold Creek. The cows were bred to be tough and aggressive to survive predators and weather conditions in the mountains, and she remembered Wade's warning that they could be nasty and bad tempered.

Tanner knew that. What on earth was the rascal thinking to go anywhere near them?

"Tanner, get back here," she yelled, but he either chose to ignore her or didn't hear over the cattle's lowing.

He moved closer to the corral, his attention fixed on something inside and Caroline had a sudden terrible foreboding that left her sick. He wouldn't go inside. He *couldn't.*

She held her breath as she raced after him but Tanner had at least a ten-yard head start. Even if he hadn't, she had learned during her time at the ranch that the boy could be quick and wily.

"Tanner Dalton, you get back here," she called again.

To her relief, this time he slowed a little and looked back at her.

"Stop," she called out.

Her relief was short-lived when he shook his head. "One of the kitties is in there," he called. "I have to get him."

She tried to see where he was looking but all she could see were milling, deadly looking hooves.

"No you don't! Let your dad go after him."

"He'll die in there and then the mommy kitty will be sad."

She was within ten feet of him now. "And if you go in there and get hurt, your dad is going to be sad *and* mad. You don't want that."

Bringing up Wade was apparently the wrong tack

completely. Even from here she could see the sudden stubborn light in the boy's eyes.

"He's already mad at me," Tanner said as he reached the corral fence.

She was close, so close, but just as she reached out to grab his shirt, he slipped under the wooden slat and was inside the pen heading toward the tiny gray kitten she could now see trembling in the middle of the milling cattle.

"Tanner, get back here," she snapped, keeping a careful eye on the cows, who were paying them no attention for now.

"I will. Soon as I get the kitty."

Caroline stood on the other side, torn about what to do. Should she go after him or go get help? She didn't know the first thing about range cattle other than they were huge and horned and scared the stuffing out of her. But she didn't dare leave even to call for Wade's help.

She had no choice. She was going to have to go after him. Oh, she was going to have a head full of gray hair by the time she made it back to Santa Cruz, she thought, then drew in one last terrified breath and slipped through the slats of the fence.

They seemed even more huge on this side of the fence, as big as small cars, and those horns looked sharp and deadly. She moved through them carefully, as slowly as she dared, her eyes on Tanner as he finally reached the tiny kitten safely after what felt like a dozen lifetimes.

"I got you," she heard him murmur, holding the little creature in his bandaged hand and stroking him with the other. "You're okay now. Nobody's going to treat you like a big baby anymore."

Caroline wanted to scream and yell and shout

Hosanna when he started toward the other side of the enclosure. She followed, doing her best to keep her body between his and the animals, who so far were paying them little heed, to her vast relief.

Twenty yards had never felt so endlessly long. Finally they were within five yards of the fence, safety almost in reach. She could taste it, feel it, even as she wondered whether she would ever be able to breathe again.

After this, she was swearing off beef forever, she decided.

They were almost there when the stupid, self-destructive kitten suddenly jumped or slipped out of Tanner's arms. He gave a cry that drew the attention of a few of the nearby animals, then went down on his hands and knees to grab it.

"Come on. We've got to get out of here," Caroline ordered.

"I know. I've almost got him. There!" he pounced on the wriggling kitten then stood up again.

Caroline grabbed for his hand—at this point she would damn well carry him *and* the blasted kitten out of here—but just as she caught his fingers, she heard a snort behind them. She turned slowly and found herself facing the beady eyes of a cow, not placid and gentle as she'd always imagined, but red-rimmed and wild and not at all happy to have them in her space.

The cow started loping toward them and Caroline's stomach dropped. "Tanner, move!" she ordered, but before the last word was out of her mouth, the cow came toward them so fast she never would have believed it if she hadn't seen it herself.

"Run!" Caroline yelled harshly and the startled boy

obeyed. She half dragged him, half carried him as they headed at full speed for the corral fence and safety.

They weren't going to make it, she realized grimly. The blasted cow would get to them a split second before they reached the fence.

She didn't think about it, she just reacted totally on instinct, picking up Tanner and the kitten and shoving him in front of her, then she pushed him through the wooden slats of the fence.

She had time only to breathe a quick, frightened prayer before the cow reached her.

When Wade caught up with that kid, he was giving him a serious lecture on following orders. A ranch could be a dangerous place for children who didn't learn early to mind their parents the first time.

If they hadn't gotten that message yet, maybe he'd been too soft on Natalie and the boys in his efforts to be as unlike his own father as possible. Tanner obviously didn't understand, so he was just going to have to drill it into the kid's head that when Wade spoke, the kid had to jump. The consequences of doing otherwise could be deadly.

He didn't have time for this today, not with the TV crew there. He almost just let Caroline deal with Tanner and his tantrum. But as he had been the one to yell at his son, he also knew he needed to be the one to explain why. They had a head start on him, though. It had taken a few minutes for him to take Cody to the outbuilding they used as a machine shop, where Seth was fixing a tractor part.

He'd given the baby to a greasy-fingered Seth, had

asked him to watch him for a minute, then had taken off after Caroline and Tanner.

As he rounded the corner of the barn, he heard a shout. He jerked his head around and his heart stuttered in his chest when he saw Caroline and Tanner in the middle of a small herd of range cows he'd culled to take to market first.

Inside the pen, Caroline's butter-yellow sweater was a small splash of color in the middle of a sea of huge russet bodies, and he could barely see Tanner.

What the hell were they doing? Did the woman not have a single brain cell in her head? He'd *told* her range cows were dangerous and here she was wandering through them like she and Tanner were tromping through a field of daisies.

At least they were heading out, he saw. They were moving toward the opposite side of the pen from where he was; he had just started around the perimeter when he saw Tanner bend down for something. A few seconds later, Caroline picked him up and headed fast toward the fence.

Just before they made it through, one of the cows got excited by the ruckus and headed toward them, head down.

His blood iced over and he yelled at them to move.

He vaulted the fence where he was, though he was still half the length of the corral away, and raced toward them, waving his hat and yelling to try to distract the angry cow.

She didn't even turn her big head, focused only on Caroline and Tanner, and Wade could do nothing but watch, horrified, as she charged.

As he ran through the milling cattle, he saw Caroline bend down and shove something through the slats—

Tanner, he realized—but an instant later the cow reached her and tossed her into the air like she was a sack full of straw.

She landed with a hideous thud against the fence and the cow lowered her head, her nostrils flared. She snorted and bawled, looking for any excuse to charge the unwanted intruder again, and Wade didn't stop to think.

He raced in front of the cow, scooped Caroline up in one arm as gently as he could under the circumstances, and used the other to haul them both up and over the fence.

He made it over to the other side just as the huge cow slammed into the fence, shaking it hard.

He felt like *he* had been the one to take that crushing hit—every ounce of oxygen in his lungs seemed to have been sucked out and, for one horrifying minute, he felt shaky and light-headed as he lowered a limp Caroline to the ground.

With effort, he forced himself to stay calm, especially as Tanner seemed hysterical enough for the both of them, his eyes huge and scared in his pale face.

"What's wrong with Caroline, Daddy? Why are her eyes closed? Is she sleeping?"

"Something like that."

"Should I go find Uncle Seth?"

"No!" With visions of all the trouble the chaos-magnet could get into on his own, Wade spoke to him sternly. "You should sit down right there and stay put."

"But I…"

He didn't have time to deal with two crises right now, not when Caroline's eyes were still closed, but he knew his son well enough to see by the obstinate jut of his jaw that a little child psychology was in order.

"Look," he tempered his tone. "I might need your help, so it would be better for Caroline's sake if you stick close to me for now, okay?"

That seemed to do the trick. Tanner nodded and settled onto the dirt outside the pens, a kitten Wade assumed to be at the heart of this whole damn fiasco still clutched tightly in his arms.

No, *he* was at the heart of this fiasco. If he hadn't yelled at Tanner, the boy wouldn't have run off and none of this would have happened.

He pushed the guilt away for now and focused on Caroline, sick all over again to see her pale, chalky features and the blue tracery of veins in her closed eyelids.

"Come on, honey. Wake up," he ordered as he did a rapid medical assessment.

Growing up on a cattle ranch had, unfortunately, given him plenty of experience in first-triage and he quickly put those skills to work. Her pulse seemed fast but strong and he hoped she had just had the wind knocked out of her.

No bones seemed to be broken but her head had taken a pretty hard crack and it wouldn't surprise him if she had a concussion. A couple of bruised or cracked ribs weren't out of the question either.

If that was the worst of it, she'd be lucky, he thought, but when he was checking her legs for fractures, he felt something sticky at the back of her thigh. He pulled his hand away and his stomach dropped when he saw it was covered in blood.

What was it from? he wondered, not sure whether he dared turn her over to see.

His mind replayed the scene in his head, relived that

sickening moment when the cow had charged, and he realized exactly what must have happened, where the blood was coming from.

The cow's horn must have caught the back of Caroline's thigh as she'd tried to get away.

He swallowed a raw oath, not wanting to scare Tanner any more than he already was, and turned her over slightly so he could see what he was dealing with.

His worst fears were confirmed at the jagged puncture wound in her thigh. Blood was already pooled underneath her and the sight made his own blood run cold.

Knowing it was vital he stop—or at least slow—the copious bleeding, he yanked off his work shirt for the relatively clean T-shirt underneath to use as a pressure bandage.

He was punching in 911 when Seth and the news crew came around the corner of the barn, probably to see what was taking him so long.

When Seth caught sight of them, of Wade without his shirt and Caroline stretched out on the ground, he hurried over, Cody in his arms.

"What happened?"

Tanner suddenly started bawling and turned to his uncle for the comfort Wade didn't have time to give.

"I went to get this k-kitty in the corral and Caroline came after me," the boy sniffled. "One of the c-cows got mad and ran to get us and Caroline pushed me out of way but the cow hurt her and now she won't wake up and it's my fault."

Seth pulled him close. "Okay. It will be okay, bud."

Wade hoped so. With all his heart, he hoped so. The

911 operator finally answered and he recognized a woman he'd gone to high school with, one of Andrea's cousins on her mother's side.

"Hey Sharon, this is Wade Dalton. I need an ambulance up here at the Cold Creek for a thirty-year-old female who's been gored by a range cow. She's unconscious, with a possible concussion and likely a couple bruised ribs as well as a puncture wound in the back of her left thigh."

"Is she breathing?"

Wade watched the steady rise and fall of her chest and took some small comfort from that. "Yeah."

"Is she out of harm's way?"

"You think I'm going to leave her in a corral with an angry cow? Yeah, she's safe. Dammit, Sharon. Just send an ambulance fast!"

"Sorry, Wade but I have to ask the questions. Stay on the line while I call the guys."

It would be at least ten minutes before the volunteer paramedics could make it here from town, he figured. A moment later, Sharon returned to the line. "Okay, they're on their way."

"Thanks, Sharon. Call Jake at the clinic, okay? Tell him it's Caroline and have him stand by."

"Will do. Want me to stay on the line until the crew gets there?"

"No. I've got it from here."

She was waking up, he saw. She moaned a little and started to move restlessly, trying to roll from her side where he'd moved her, to her back. He held her still and he watched her eyes blink open as she tried to get her bearings.

He saw the pain and confusion in her eyes as she looked blankly at the camera crew and Seth, then she turned her head slightly, probably so she could see what was keeping her from rolling back.

The minute her gaze found him, the distress in her features eased and her body seemed to relax.

"I guess I wasn't fast enough," she murmured.

"Told you those range cows can be ornery buggers."

He was astonished at the tenderness soaking through him, though it couldn't quite crowd out all the fear.

She closed her eyes for a moment but opened them a second later and he saw they were wide and panicky. "Tanner! Where's Tanner?"

"Over there with Seth, see? All safe and sound."

She followed the direction he pointed and the relief in her eyes touched some deep chord inside him. She was battered and bloody, but her first thought was still for his son.

At the sound of his name, Tanner approached them, his cheeks tearstained. He knelt down and grabbed hold of Caroline's hand. "Are you mad at me?"

"Oh, honey. Of course not." She squeezed his fingers and Wade felt like some icy band around his heart he hadn't realized was there had started to loosen.

"I'm sorry I went inside the pens where I'm not supposed to go. I'm sorry you got hurt."

"How's the kitten?"

"Good."

He held it up for her and she sighed. "A lot of trouble for a little ball of fur. Good thing he's cute."

The T-shirt Wade was using as a bandage was soaked with blood and he could see her features were getting paler. The kids didn't need to see all this, he thought, and he had a feeling Caroline would feel more comfortable without the crowd of onlookers.

"Seth, maybe you should take the boys and our guests up to the house until the ambulance gets here."

"You sure there's nothing we can do?"

"Send somebody back with something clean I can use as a fresh bandage."

Seth nodded and herded everyone toward the house.

When they were gone, Wade folded his work shirt and tucked it under her cheek so she didn't have to lie in the dirt.

"Thank you," she murmured, her voice weak and thready.

"Hang on. The ambulance is on its way."

Her eyes fluttered open and connected with his. "Oh, is that really necessary? I don't want to be a bother."

"Honey, you've been gored by an eight-hundred-pound range cow. Trust me, it's necessary."

She blinked and the pain in her eyes tore at his heart. He would do anything to take it away, but he was completely helpless. "Gored," she murmured. "That must be why my leg feels like it's on fire."

"Afraid so."

"I thought I just went the rounds with a freight train."

"Yeah, a close encounter with a cow will do that to you."

"You sound like you speak from experience."

"A few times. You can't grow up on a ranch without your share of bumps and bruises."

"Have you been gored?"

She was talking to distract herself from the pain, he realized, and he felt another band around his heart loosen.

"Once. I was fourteen and Jake dared me to do a little bull riding. Dad had this ornery bull he was selling to one of the neighbors, so he had it penned waiting for them to come for it. Somehow we managed to chase him into a chute and I climbed on. We didn't have a rope or anything, just me being an idiot. I probably lasted half a second before I went flying into the air. I was like you, I almost made it out before he caught me."

The worst part of the whole ordeal had been Hank's fury when he'd found they had used an expensive animal for sport. He hadn't worried so much about his son as he had about the bull. Hank had even made him walk up to the house through agonizing pain, he remembered.

Marjorie had almost left the bastard over that one, he remembered, then he realized Caroline's eyes were closed again and pushed the memory away.

"Come on, honey. Hang on."

"Hurts."

He brushed her hair out of her eyes. "I know, sweetheart. But listen, there's the ambulance. Can you hear it? They'll be here in a minute to take you to Jake and he'll fix you right up. He's a hell of a doctor."

"Will you come with me?"

Her quiet words ripped out what was left of his heart. "I doubt they'll let me ride on the ambulance but I'll bring the boys and follow it to the clinic, okay?"

She nodded just as the ambulance arrived.

A moment later, the place bustled with paramedics. Wade stood up, shirtless and suddenly freezing in the cool wind.

His hands were bloody, his chest ached, and he felt like he'd aged at least ten years in the last ten minutes.

Chapter Twelve

Two hours later, Wade decided he'd aged more like twenty years since seeing that cow heading straight for Caroline and Tanner.

Now he sat across the desk from his brother in Jake's pathologically clean office at the clinic, where Wade had sat for the last two hours thumbing through journal articles on topics about which he had no interest or comprehension.

"So what can you tell me? Are you done with her yet? Will she have to transfer to the hospital in Idaho Falls or can I take her back to the Cold Creek?"

Jake leaned back in his chair twirling a pen in both hands with something perilously close to a smirk on his features. "I'm afraid that as you're not a blood relative of Ms. Montgomery, I'm not at liberty to give you any information about her condition unless she signs a release."

He glared. "I'm *your* relative and I can still pound your smart ass into the ground without breaking a sweat."

"Sorry, but self-preservation is not adequate justification for me to break the law. Bring it on, brother."

Wade suddenly remembered just why Jake used to drive him crazy when they were kids. "You're enjoying this, aren't you?"

"You've been pacing in here like a nervous father for the last two hours. I have to say, I haven't seen you this upset since..." His voice trailed off, along with his grin, and his mouth tightened.

"Since Andrea's illness," Wade finished for him grimly.

Compassion and regret flashed across Jake's features. "I'm sorry for giving you a hard time. I wasn't thinking about how all this must bring back memories of Andi."

"It's not the same. Andi was my wife. My life. Caroline is just...just..."

He couldn't seem to come up with the right word for the place she had filled in his life. Sometimes he wasn't even sure he liked her very much, then others he couldn't stop thinking about her, remembering that kiss they had shared, her crooked little smile that seemed to brighten the whole house, her endless patience with his kids.

Despite his protestations to Jake, he had to admit that his emotions of the last two hours had been eerily similar to those terrible, helpless days he had prowled that hospital room in Idaho Falls while his wife had tried and failed to fight off the infection that had finally claimed her life.

How could he even compare the two experiences? It made no sense and yet his worry and fear felt the same.

"Caroline's a trooper," Jake said. "No tears, no hysterics. She even made a few jokes while she was under the local and I was sewing up the puncture wound. Forty-five stitches, all told, but she's doing fine."

"I thought you couldn't talk about her condition with me."

Jake pulled a paper out of a file and tossed it on the desk, his expression a little shamefaced. "Oh, look. A release form. I must have forgotten Connie had her sign it when they were filling out her insurance papers."

Wade glared at him in disgust. "You always were a son of a bitch."

Jake smirked. "How could I be otherwise when I had such a fine example in my older brother?"

"So what can you tell me? What's the extent of her injuries?"

Jake suddenly became all doctor, no longer a teasing younger brother trying to yank his chain. "Your triage assessment was right on. The X-rays showed two cracked ribs, just as you suspected, I'm guessing from hitting the fence. From what I can piece together, the cow came at her from behind, head down, and caught her in the leg."

"Yeah, I know that part. I was there."

Just remembering it sent cold chills down his spine. He knew he would never forget that horrible moment when she'd gone flying through the air. No doubt he would relive it in his nightmares for a long time.

"Well, she was relatively lucky. It could have been much worse. As it is, she has a deep laceration in the back of her thigh. It went through the biceps femoris but missed the popliteal artery by a fraction of an inch. If it hadn't, she probably would have bled to death at the Cold Creek before you were able to summon help."

Wade felt cold, light-headed, just thinking about the idea of a world without Caroline in it.

How had she come to be so important to him in just a few days? He let out a ragged breath then covered it by coughing a little as if he were only clearing his throat.

"What kind of a recovery time is she looking at?"

Jake studied him closely and Wade hoped like hell none of his emotions were showing on his face.

"Well, I can't lie to you, she's going to hurt for several days. The ribs are going to be the worst of it but deep tissue trauma like a gore wound isn't easy to bounce back from."

"Yeah, I remember."

"That's right, I forgot you've been there, El Matador."

He narrowed his gaze. "You should be damn grateful you're a good doctor, otherwise you'd be too obnoxious to tolerate."

Jake laughed, unoffended. "We gave her a local anesthetic while I was sewing things up and she's still a little numb from that but I don't think there's any need to transfer her to Idaho Falls to the hospital. I can keep a closer eye on her here. She'll have to stay off it completely for a couple days and I've urged her not to travel for at least a week. I figured she can stay at my place until she's ready to go back to California. I can take turns checking on her throughout the day with my clinic nurses."

"Forget it. She's staying at the Cold Creek."

His vehemence seemed to surprise Jake as much as it did him.

He wasn't sure why he hated the idea of her staying with his brother so much. It probably made more sense all around. She would certainly be able to get more rest without his kids in the way and she would be closer to expert care with Jake in the same house, but he hated the whole idea.

Jake folded his arms. "And why is that? Because, as usual, you think you're responsible for the whole world?"

"Not the whole world. Just people who are injured on *my* ranch, by one of *my* cows, while they happen to be in the process of saving *my* son's life. I'd say that gives me some responsibility to see she's cared for properly."

"You don't think she would be at my house? See that diploma on the wall? I do happen to be the doctor here, remember?"

"As if you would ever let me forget. But just because you're the one with the fancy degree doesn't automatically make you the best one to take care of Caroline," he said. "You work eighteen-hour days and she would be alone all day except for the few times you sent people to check on her. She'd be miserable."

"You're a great one to talk about working long hours! Your kids see you for five minutes a day if they're lucky."

What was it with everybody telling him what a lousy father he was, all of a sudden?

"Look," Jake went on, "I'm sure Caroline understands you're grateful to her for going after Tanner like that. But she also has to know you have your hands more than full at the Cold Creek. I haven't forgotten how crazy autumns on the ranch can be. And with Caroline on the injured list, you're back to where you were when Mom left, without anybody to help you with the kids."

Wade clenched his teeth. "I'm well aware of that, but thanks for the reminder."

"I'm only pointing out that you can't handle the load you've already got. What makes you think you can take on the care of an injured woman, too?"

"We'll manage. I'll just have to take a few days off."

Jake stared at him like a fat, wriggling trout had just popped out the top of his head. "A few days off what?"

He shrugged. "Seth can handle things around the ranch and I'll stick close to the house and take care of Caroline and the boys until she's back on her feet."

He braced himself for more arguments but whatever his brother threw at him, Wade refused to let himself be deterred. He had absolutely no intention of letting Caroline recover anywhere but at the Cold Creek.

He owed her this for what she had done for Tanner—hell, what she'd done for all of them the last six days. She had stepped up when he needed help and he couldn't do any less for her.

Something else had been bothering him these last two hours and Jake bringing up Andi's illness finally helped him crystallize it in his mind.

When his wife had been so sick, he could do nothing for her but haunt the hospital, hound the doctors and spend every spare minute on his knees praying for God not to take her.

He was a man used to doing, not sitting back and watching others, and it had been hell to stand by while his wife had grown sicker and sicker.

Here was something concrete he could handle, something he hadn't been given the chance to do for

Andi. And maybe by helping to nurse Caroline, in some way, another of the scars crisscrossing his heart might heal.

"I'm taking her home," he said firmly.

To his surprise, Jake—the same one Marjorie used to say would argue with her if she said his eyes were blue—completely folded.

After another long look at Wade, he nodded. "Fine. I'll give you a list of discharge instructions before you take her back to the ranch. She's being fitted for a pair of crutches and I'll have to call in a prescription for painkillers and heavy-duty antibiotics, then after that she should be good to go."

Despite his relief at not having to engage in hand-to-hand combat with his brother over the rights to care for her, he suddenly felt a spurt of panic at the task in front of him.

"Just like that? Are you sure you don't need to keep her longer for observation or something?"

Jake seemed to be fighting a smile. "Oh, I think I've seen all I need to see."

"What's that supposed to mean?" he snapped.

"Oh, nothing." Jake stood up, stretching a little as he did. His surgical scrubs were sweat-stained and he suddenly looked as tired as if he'd spent all day in the saddle roping steers.

"Never mind," Jake said. "I'll go let the nurses know you're ready."

Ready? He wasn't sure he'd go that far. Still, he'd made his choice and he backed his words up with action.

Hours later, Caroline dragged herself out of an uneasy, pill-induced sleep to a muted bass voice, a higher-pitched whisper and pain in every single molecule of her body.

Mercy, she hurt. For several moments after she awoke, she concentrated only on breathing past the pain until she could think straight. Even breathing hurt and she couldn't figure out why until she remembered the cracked ribs. Wade's brother had warned her they would probably hurt worse than anything else at first and she discovered he'd been telling the truth.

Her leg burned and throbbed but she could endure that. What she hated was not being able to take a deep breath into her lungs for the pain.

She did the best she could, keeping her eyes closed while she focused. Through the layers of pain, she listened to the voices—Wade and Tanner, she realized.

"If you can't remember to whisper, you'll have to leave," Wade admonished his son.

"I'll be quiet, I promise," Tanner said and Caroline almost smiled at that impossible claim. She wasn't sure Tanner could be quiet even if his mouth were taped shut.

Her eyelids were just about the only part of her that wasn't sore right about now, so she propped one up just enough to see she was alone with Wade and Tanner in a room she recognized as one of the empty bedrooms on the main floor.

Nat and Cody were nowhere in sight but Wade sat at the old-fashioned writing desk in the room with Tanner on his lap. The boy had a blueberry-colored crayon in his hand—his *unbandaged* hand, she saw with some delight, and his cute little face wore a frown of concentration, his tongue clamped between his teeth, as he peered down at what he was coloring.

"You sure you want that horse's tail to be blue?" Wade asked, his voice low.

"Do you think I should change it?"

"I guess it's your horse so you can do whatever you want. If you want it to be pink with purple polka dots, have at it."

"It's for Caroline, not for me, and she likes blue. She told me. It reminds her of the ocean in the summer. She lives by the ocean, did you know that?"

"I did."

"I asked her if she could go swimming anytime she wants and she said the water is kind of cold where she lives but she still likes to walk on the beach and look for seashells and sand dollars and take her shoes off so she can jump over the little waves."

"That sounds fun."

"And she said we could come visit her sometime in California and she would take us to find starfish and stuff. Can we, Dad?"

"We'll see," Wade whispered, an odd look in his eyes. "Looks like you're about done there."

"Yeah. It's a get-better card. Grandma and me made one for Molly Johnson when she had the chicken pox. You think Caroline will like it?"

Before she could answer that of course she would, she saw Wade give a slow smile then kiss the top of Tanner's head. "She'll love it because you made it for her," he said in that same low voice.

As she studied those two male heads so close together, one so masculine and dark and strong, the other small and darling, Caroline's pain faded for just a moment, overwhelmed by a stunning realization.

She was in love with him.

It poured over her, through her, an inexorable, undeniable wash of emotion.

In love with Wade Dalton. Of all the idiotic things for her to do!

Her chest hurt, but she was certain the pain had nothing to do with her cracked ribs and everything to do with her cracked head. She had to be crazy to let things come to this.

What was she thinking? Why hadn't she protected herself better? Made some effort to toughen her spine, her mind, her heart?

She tried to tell herself that was just the painkiller talking, giving her all kinds of weird delusions, but she couldn't quite make herself buy that explanation.

The worst of it was realizing she'd been sliding down this precarious path a little more each moment since she'd arrived at the Cold Creek. Surely she could have switched direction at some point along the journey if only she'd been awake enough to see in front of herself.

She had ignored the signs along the way, unwilling to face the truth until she'd been literally knocked off her feet.

Oh, this was bad. Seriously bad. She was going to end up more battered and broken by loving Wade Dalton than just a few paltry cracked ribs and a gouged thigh.

She thought of the article Darci Perez had mentioned earlier in the afternoon, another lifetime ago, it seemed. "Top Ten Best Ways to Guarantee a Happy, Fulfilling Life."

She had written it several months ago and couldn't remember everything in it but she was fairly sure that nowhere in there did she mention that one of those ways to guarantee happiness was to fall head over heels for a workaholic rancher who didn't trust her, didn't like her, and who was still grieving for his late wife.

She must have made some sound of distress—she wasn't entirely sure but she must have done something to draw attention because both of the males at the writing table swiveled their heads in her direction at the same time.

"Caroline! You're awake!" Tanner beamed with delight.

Wade studied her intently and she flushed, praying her emotions weren't exposed somehow for all to see. He approached the bed and she dug her fingers into the quilt.

"Did we wake you?" he asked. "We tried to be quiet but I'm afraid that was a losing battle."

Her mouth suddenly felt as if she'd been chewing sandpaper in her sleep and she could do nothing but shake her head.

He instinctively seemed to sense her need. From the bedside table next to her, he picked up a pitcher and ice rattled as he poured a glass of water and handed it to her. She took it gratefully and sipped until she thought she might be able to squeeze out a word or two.

"Thank you," she murmured and her voice sounded rough, scratchy.

How long had she been sleeping? she wondered. It was dark and Tanner was in pajamas, so it must have been more than a few hours.

"How do you feel?" Wade asked when she lowered the glass.

"Like I should have tire tread marks somewhere on my person."

He gave a sympathetic smile. "No tread marks that I can see. Maybe a hoofprint or two."

She winced and tried to move to a more comfortable position. She realized as she moved that she was wearing her nightgown. She frowned trying to remember how she had changed out of the clothes she'd been wearing when she'd been gored, but she couldn't grab hold of it.

She had worn what was left of her clothes home from the clinic, hadn't she? Much of the afternoon felt like a big blur. Someone here at the ranch had to have helped her change into her nightgown. Wade? she wondered and flushed at the thought.

"Where are the others?" she asked to distract herself.

"Cody didn't have much of a nap so he crashed right after dinner. And Nat's in doing homework."

"What time is it?"

"Almost eight. I gave this one a few more minutes but it's just about bedtime for him, too."

Tanner walked to the side of the bed, his picture in his outstretched hand. "I made you a get-better card."

He set it carefully on the quilt and she picked it up, touched by his effort. "It's beautiful. I especially like the blue tail on the horse."

He grinned at his dad. "See? Told you she'd like it!"

Wade rubbed his hair. "So you did. Maybe Caroline would like us to tape it up somewhere that she could see it all the time. How about there by the bed?"

"Perfect," she said as Tanner rummaged in the desk and emerged triumphant with some tape. The next few minutes were spent watching him hang it crookedly on the wall.

"Thank you so much," she exclaimed when it was done. "You know what? It's working! I feel better already."

He beamed and fluttered his hands. "Hey, guess what? Uncle Jake took off my bandage when he came to check on you a while ago and he said I could leave it off since it's looking good."

"Great news!"

"Yeah, and I can get it wet and everything! I had a bath and I could play with my boats with both hands."

Wade stepped in and placed a hand on the boy's shoulder. "Okay, bud. Time to hit the sack. We've got a big day tomorrow."

Something important was happening the next day. She knew it but she couldn't seem to grab hold of what that might be.

"We're gonna play basketball and clean out the toy box and maybe make brownies if Dad can figure out how."

No, that wasn't it. She closed her eyes but still couldn't figure it out.

When she opened them, Wade was watching her, his blue eyes dark with concern.

"Go on up and find a book and I'll be up to read to you in a minute," he told his son.

The boy nodded, then smiled. "Night, Caroline."

She reached out and squeezed his fingers. "Good night."

Tanner hesitated for a moment by her bedside then, before she knew what he intended, he bent over and kissed her cheek, leaving behind the sweet smell of just-washed little boy.

"Thanks for helping me save the kitten. I would have been sad if a cow stepped on her but I'm real sorry you got hurt."

"Me, too. But I'm glad you were safe."

After Tanner left, Wade pulled his chair to her side, watching her with a strange, inscrutable expression on his face.

"You need another pain pill. I'm on strict orders to make you eat something before you take one. I can't claim to be a great cook but Mom left some soup in the freezer and I can heat you some. Beef barley."

She didn't want to eat and she certainly didn't want another pill. But already the pain was building and she knew it would only get worse if she didn't take something for it.

"I'm sorry to be a bother," she said. "I know you have so much to do…."

Suddenly it hit her and she remembered the scene with the TV crew that had led up to her accident. "The interview. You've got the news interview tomorrow. You don't have time to babysit me."

"It's all under control," he assured her.

"How?"

"Don't worry about it. I'm going to go in and warm up some soup for you then you can take a pill and rest."

She laid back on the pillow, too weak and sore and heartsick to argue.

Chapter Thirteen

Twenty-four hours after leaving the clinic, Caroline felt as if that blow to the head she'd taken had permanently jostled her brain.

Either that or she had somehow slipped through the rabbit hole into some alternate universe.

She studied Wade standing in the doorway with a tray of more of the ubiquitous soup and scarcely recognized him. Who was this man and what had he done with the distant, taciturn rancher she'd come to know since arriving at the Cold Creek?

Wade had been nothing but solicitous and concerned since her accident. All day he had played nursemaid, fetching and carrying and even just sitting with her.

She had awakened in the night from a terrible dream where a vast herd of cows with glowing red eyes chased her down the beach, their heads down and their horns swinging until she had no choice but to dive into the surf to evade those vicious horns.

When she jerked her eyes open, gasping for breath, she found Wade dozing in the chair, his stocking feet propped on the bed beside her and a ranching magazine open across his chest.

She found him surprisingly vulnerable in sleep, without the hard edges and harsh lines on his features during the day.

Without the burdens and cares he carried when awake, he looked young, relaxed, and she grieved for this man who had lost so much and who could only release the load of his responsibilities while he slept.

She watched him for a long time, wondering how many opportunities she would have to share this kind of quiet moment with him. Her feelings for him were a heavy ache in her chest and she wondered what she would possibly do with them after she left the Cold Creek.

Sometime during her scrutiny, his eyes opened and she was completely disarmed when his cheeks colored and he dropped his stocking feet to the carpet.

"Sorry." He rubbed a hand through his hair. "Guess I fell asleep."

"What are you doing here?" she asked.

He shrugged. "You've had a concussion. I'm supposed to check on you through the night."

"I don't think that requires an all-night vigil, do you?"

"I promised Jake I would follow orders. He said to keep an eye on you through the night, so that's what I'm doing. Or that's what I'm supposed to be doing anyway. I won't fall asleep again."

Completely astonished, she stared at him, not knowing how to respond. "You can't stay up all night! I'm sure that's not what Jake meant. Tomorrow's a big day for you, with the TV interview and all. You need your sleep."

He closed the magazine and set it on the desk, not meeting her gaze. "Seth and I decided he would take care of the interview. He knows as much as I do about ranch operations. They shot plenty of footage of me spouting off today before your accident. I told Darci the reporter will just have to use that if he wants me included in the story."

Maybe if her brain weren't so fuzzy from the pain and the pills, she could figure this out. As it was, nothing he was saying made sense. "So you're not going to do the interview?"

"No. Seth is."

"But why? This is an important opportunity for you to showcase the Cold Creek and the improvements you've made."

"Yeah, and Seth can do that as well as I can. Better, probably. He's young, good-looking and has a hell of a lot more charm. All that will play well on camera."

She wondered if Wade had any idea that while Seth was extremely good-looking and probably flirted in his sleep, he reminded her of a young, playful pup compared to his older brother.

Wade was rugged, masculine, *compelling*. No woman who saw him on or off camera would ever be able to forget him.

Why had Wade suddenly decided to delegate the important interview to his brother?

While she tried to puzzle it out, she shifted to find a better position and wanted to smack her forehead when the answer came to her.

Her. He was doing this because of her. "You think you need to stay here and babysit me. *That's* why you're having Seth do the interview."

"Don't worry about it. We've got everything worked out."

"I will worry about it. I can't let you make that kind of sacrifice for me. I can take care of myself, Wade."

"You can't even get out of bed by yourself right now."

"You don't have to feel responsible for me!"

"I *am* responsible for you."

"Since when?"

He met her glare with a level look. "Since you nearly died saving my son's life."

She let out a breath, embarrassed by the depth of gratitude in his eyes. "Don't be silly. You don't owe me a thing."

"I owe you *everything.*" His voice, low and intense, sent shivers down her spine. "If you hadn't been there, Tanner would have been trampled or worse in that corral."

"Wade—"

"No sense arguing about it. Seth is going to take over for me for a few days while the kids and I get you back on your feet. That includes doing the interview."

A few days? Wade Dalton was taking time off work during what she had quickly come to learn was his busiest time of the year for *her?*

"I… You can't do that."

"It's done." Suddenly he gave her a disarming smile. If she weren't already in bed, he would have knocked the pins right out from under her with it. "Besides, my mother—your new stepmother—would never forgive me if I didn't take proper care of you, especially with the circumstances of how you were injured. I can hear her now lecturing me all about bad karma and all that. Now let's get you something for the pain I can tell is coming back nastier than a one-legged dog with fleas."

She hadn't known how to answer him the night before and she still didn't know what to say as she studied him in the doorway, the boys on either side of him. Tanner held a pitcher in his hand and Cody had what she assumed was an empty plastic cup.

"Lunch time." Wade smiled.

"Hi, Caroline," Tanner chirped. "We made soup and a cheese san'wich. My dad made it and everything."

Wade shrugged, his cheeks suspiciously ruddy. "I opened a can and threw a piece of cheese and bread under the broiler. Sorry, but that's about the best I can do unless I'm standing in front of a barbecue grill."

"I'm sure it will be delicious," she said.

"Sit by Care." The youngest Dalton beamed, holding his arms up for her.

"You'll have to have your dad help you up," she told Cody.

Wade set the tray on the table by the bed. "Better not. He might bump your ribs or your leg."

"Then I'll scream bloody murder and hand him back to you."

He shook his head. "It's your funeral."

He lifted the toddler up and Cody gave her a big, toothy smile like he hadn't seen her in months. He held out his arms and hugged her, tucking his head beneath her chin. It did hurt but she decided a little pain was a small price to pay to hold a sweet, loving little boy who smelled of sunshine and baby lotion.

"Hey Dad, can I sit up there with Caroline, too?" Tanner asked.

"You'd better not. You're a little bigger and tougher than your brother."

Tanner's heart didn't seem to be broken by that news. "Well, can I go back and watch *Blue's Clues* then?"

Wade considered. "Stay by the TV, though. No wandering around outside and no going in the kitchen."

"Okay," Tanner promised and hurried out of the room with a quick wave to Caroline.

"Can you eat like that?" Wade asked.

Caroline settled the boy next to her, on the other side from her injured leg. "We'll be just fine, won't we, Cody?"

The toddler nodded and cuddled closer. To her surprise, Wade pulled up a chair while she tackled her lunch.

"You don't have to stay," she murmured, a little uncomfortable at him watching her eat.

"I'd better, just so I can keep the kid there from giving you a judo chop to the leg."

"He's fine. I think he's going to be asleep in a minute."

Sure enough, before she even tasted her soup, his eyes were half-closed and a moment later he was out for the count. He moved a little closer, bumping her leg, but she wasn't about to complain.

"He's a beautiful boy," she said with a smile. "All three of your children are. You know, I can see bits of you in Nat and Tanner but Cody is his own little man."

She paused, debating the merits of pressing forward, then took the plunge anyway. "From what I can tell, he resembles the pictures I've seen of your late wife."

Wade said nothing for a long moment, then he nodded slowly. "He does. If you looked at baby pictures of Andrea, you would swear you're looking at Cody. She had the same brown eyes and blond hair, the same dimples, the same full bottom lip."

He paused. "And you know, their personalities are similar in a lot of ways. He's got the same sunny disposition and same easygoing attitude toward life. I'm sure you've noticed Cody is a cuddler and Andrea was happiest when we were all sprawled together on the couch watching a movie."

She smiled, touched that he would share this piece of his past with her. "What a wonderful blessing that you've been given these three beautiful children so you can remember your wife whenever you look at them. Especially this one."

"They are a blessing. Every one of them." He paused, a faraway look in his eyes. Not pain, precisely. Just memories.

When he spoke, his voice was low and she sensed instinctively he was telling her something he didn't share easily.

"I couldn't even look at Cody for a week or so after Andi's death," he said slowly. "It was such a crazy time and I was...lost inside. Totally messed up. My wife was gone and here was this bawling newborn baby who needed so much, along with Tanner who wasn't much more than a baby himself and Natalie who was old enough to know what was going on."

"She must have been devastated."

"We all were. This sounds awful," he went on, "but I kept thinking, I hadn't wanted another one in the first place. I'd been perfectly content with Natalie and Tanner. Andi was the one who wanted another child. I guess part of me blamed Cody. It wasn't fair, I know, but I thought, if not for him, she wouldn't have caught that staph infection during the delivery. She would have been healthy and strong, ready to take on the world, like always. My other two kids would have still had their mother, I still would have had a wife. If only she hadn't pushed so hard to have another one, everything would be just fine. I don't know if I blamed God, Andi or the baby more for her death."

"Oh, Wade."

He looked at the boy and the softness in his eyes brought tears to her own.

"Thank the Lord my Mom stepped in to help because I wanted nothing to do with him. I don't think I would have let him starve but I sure didn't want to see him or touch him or anything. But about a week after the funeral, Mom was in taking a shower when Cody woke up howling. I almost left the house right then, I couldn't stand it, but I finally made myself go in to see what he needed."

She almost reached for his hand but she didn't want to move, to breathe, afraid any interruption might compel him to stop talking. He was giving her a rare window into his world and she was touched beyond words that he would share this with her.

"It was like something out of the movies. You know, one of those unbelievable moments." He smiled a little. "One minute he's shrieking loud enough to knock the house over, but as soon as he caught sight of me, he shut right up, stuck a little fist in his mouth and just stared at me out of Andi's eyes for the longest time."

He didn't add that when Marjorie had finally come in to check on the quiet baby after her shower, she'd found Wade in the rocking chair clutching Cody tightly and bawling his eyes out like he hadn't been able to do since Andi's death.

He also didn't add that in those first horrible months after she'd died, the only peaceful moments he remembered—the moments he'd somehow felt closest to Andi—were when he'd been holding their baby. On nights when he couldn't sleep for the pain, he even used to sometimes go into Cody's room in the middle of the night, just so he could pick the sleeping baby up out of his crib and rock him until he could remember how to breathe again around the vast, endless grief.

He looked up from his thoughts to find Caroline watching him, a tear trickling down her cheek. Guilt swamped him. "You're in pain and I'm in here yakking your leg off. I'm sorry."

She reached out and squeezed his arm, and the simple touch almost made him feel like bawling, too, for some crazy reason.

"No. I'm fine," she insisted. "I just can't imagine what it must have been like for you."

She was crying for *him?* He wasn't exactly sure how he felt about that but he did know that when she pulled her hand away, part of him wanted to reach for it again.

"The hardest thing was the kids. It still is, really," he said. "Trying to do right by them is tough on my own, even with Marjorie's help. Whatever you might think—whatever my mom thinks—I love my kids. They're first in my heart, even if I don't always act like it. Everything I do is for them. I might not be able to give them as much time as I should, but I love them."

He heard that blasted defensiveness creep into his voice, but he couldn't seem to help it. He wanted so much for her to understand. It seemed suddenly vitally important that she not see him as a father trying to shirk his duty by his children.

She wiped at her eyes. "I know you do. I know. It was presumptuous of me to ever imply otherwise and I'm sorry for what I said the other night. I have this bad habit of thinking I know what everyone in the entire world should be doing to improve their lives. I forget that my help isn't always wanted or needed."

"I guess that's why you're a life coach, then. So people will pay you to boss them around."

She laughed softly at that and, for some reason, it moved him that she could still laugh even when she was in pain—and at herself, no less.

"My dad always told me that if you're lucky enough to find something you're good at, you have to hang on to it with both hands and not let go no matter what the world throws at you."

He decided in the spirit of goodwill between them, he would put aside his animosity toward her father and try to understand what his mother might have seen in the guy.

"What does your father do for a living? I never thought to ask Marjorie. I guess that's something I should know if I'm to perform my son-in-law duties effectively."

What had he said to put that strange, edgy light in her eyes? he wondered.

"Oh, he's retired," she said quickly.

"From what?"

Her fingers tightened on the quilt. "A little of everything. Sales, support, research and development. I guess mostly sales, you could say."

Now that sounded like a whole lot of nothing. He wanted to push for more specifics but he could plainly tell she was uncomfortable with the subject and he didn't want to press her when she was hurting.

He didn't want their conversation to end, though, he realized, so he fished around for another subject.

"Where are you from originally? I assumed California but I just realized I never bothered to ask."

Again, he got the strange impression she was picking her words carefully. "I'm one of those unfortunate people who doesn't really have a hometown, except the one I've chosen for myself as an adult."

She smiled a little but it didn't reach as far as her eyes. "I'm not like you, born and bred in one place like the Cold Creek. We lived in Texas for a while when I was a kid—Houston and San Antonio, mostly—and then my mother died when I was eight and after that we moved around a lot."

"Just your dad and you?"

She gave a sharp, tight-looking nod and he wondered if she was hurting. "I was an only child."

"I'm sorry."

She looked surprised at his word. "When I was a kid, other kids at school always told me how lucky I was to have my dad all to myself. But I always wanted a couple of older brothers and an older sister or two."

"My brothers drive me crazy most of the time but I can't imagine not having either of them."

"You're very lucky," she murmured. "And your children are as well. No matter what else happens, you all have each other."

"You have your dad," he pointed out.

She seemed to find that amusing in a strange sort of way. "Right. My dad."

"And according to Seth, you're now our stepsister."

He meant it as a joke to lighten her odd mood but she gave him a long, charged look that had his palms sweating.

"I don't think either one of us wants to think very seriously about that, do you?" she said quietly.

He suddenly couldn't think of anything but the kiss they had shared, of her arms wrapped around him, of the wild heat flashing between them like a summer lightning storm.

He shifted, wishing he could get those blasted images out of his head. But every time he looked at her mouth, every time she smiled, every time her soft vanilla scent drifted to him, they came flooding back.

The room instantly seemed to seethe with tension and he regretted the loss of their brief camaraderie.

He had never told anyone about Cody, probably because he was ashamed of that initial anger he'd felt toward a helpless, completely innocent little baby. Marjorie was the only one with any inkling and even she didn't know the whole of it.

He wasn't sure why he'd told Caroline, he only knew that once the words had started, he couldn't seem to hold them back.

He had learned a few things about her but he wanted more. He wanted to know everything. The name of her second-grade teacher, her favorite kind of candy bar, her happiest memory.

The realization scared the hell out of him. He had no need to know those things about Caroline Montgomery—or to share his deepest, innermost secrets with her.

That was the kind of thing a man did with a woman he was dating, a woman he thought he might have feelings for.

A woman whose kiss he couldn't get out of his head.

Wade rose abruptly. "I'd better go check on Tanner. Who knows what kind of trouble he might get into if I don't."

"Right. Good idea," she said, her voice quiet.

"Do you want me to take Cody out of your way?"

"No. Let him sleep."

Her smile looked a little strained, he thought with concern. "Are you sure he's not hurting you?"

"He's fine," she insisted, running a gentle hand over Cody's blond curls. The boy made a sound and moved closer. "I'll call if I need you to come get him."

He nodded, picked up the lunch tray and headed for the door, wondering as he went how on earth he could be so jealous of a two-year-old.

Chapter Fourteen

By the afternoon of the second day after her injury, Caroline decided she'd had enough of pain pills that left her loopy and disconnected, and she stopped taking them, at least during the day.

Though the result was a low, throbbing ache in her ribs and stabbing pain in her leg, she decided it was worth the price to feel moderately like herself again.

She also reached the firm conclusion that if she had to spend one more moment in her room—lovely though it was—she just might have to throw one of her crutches through the window.

She nearly planted a big, juicy kiss on Jake when he came to check on her and said there was no reason she couldn't sit on one of the recliners in the great room with Wade and the children.

"Those sore ribs are going to make it tough to work the crutches," Jake said. "I'll go get Wade so he can help you move to the other room."

Before she could ask Jake why *he* couldn't help her, he left with a peculiar smirk on his handsome features.

She hadn't seen much of Wade since their encounter the day before. She couldn't decide if he was avoiding her or simply wrapped up in the children and the ranch paperwork she knew he tried to catch up on anytime he had a spare minute.

He had brought her meals and checked every hour or so to see if she needed anything—or sent one of the kids in to check—but there had been no more opportunities for revealing conversations.

She was glad, she told herself. She was afraid she had already revealed too much about herself. Better if he left her alone so she had no more opportunity to make a fool of herself or to slide deeper and deeper in love with him.

For an instant, she regretted asking Jake if she could start getting up and around. Maybe she should stay in her room, despite the boredom, for the sake of her heart.

The decision was taken out of her hands a moment later, though, when Wade walked through the open doorway. He wore jeans and a soft gray chamois shirt, and he looked big and hard and gorgeous.

She sighed, wishing she were wearing something a little more attractive than her old nightgown and robe.

"I'm under orders to help you into the other room," he said, gazing at some point above her head.

"Jake is afraid I'm not quite ready to handle the crutches on my own because of the bruised ribs."

For some reason, she was compelled to make it clear

to him this had been entirely his brother's idea that Wade come in to help her.

Wade finally met her gaze and her stomach twirled a little at the strange expression in his eyes. She would have given just about anything right at that moment to know what was going on inside his head.

He moved toward the bed and, before she realized what he was doing, he scooped her up gingerly. Not expecting the move, or the sudden shock of finding herself held so gently in his powerful arms, she couldn't contain a quick gasp.

"Did I hurt you?" He looked aghast at the idea.

"No. I just don't think this was what Jake meant!"

A muscle flexed in his jaw. "Oh, I'm pretty sure it was, since his exact words were *go carry Caroline from her bedroom to the recliner in the great room.*"

"He should have at least warned me what the master plan was here," she said.

"Yeah, me, too," she thought she heard him mutter but it was so low she couldn't be sure.

"I can probably make it on the crutches if you'll just spot me," she said, though she wanted nothing more than to stay right here, nestled into his heat and strength.

He smelled divine, of some kind of outdoorsy aftershave, and his shirt had to be the softest material she'd ever felt as her arms slid around his neck to hang on. He was close enough that she could have drawn his head down to hers without much effort at all....

"You could have said something if you were bored in there."

She blinked, hoping he didn't notice the sudden color she could feel creeping over her features. "I didn't want to bother you. You're already doing so much for me."

"What? A few meals, that's about it. Doesn't seem like much in return for saving my son's life."

Before she could respond to that, they made their way far too quickly to the great room.

The moment they walked through the doorway, the children reacted in different ways to the sight of her in their father's arms. The boys both shrieked her name as if they hadn't seen her in months and raced to her side.

While she was greeting them with laughter, she caught sight of Natalie sitting at the table with Jake, her math book spread out in front of her. She looked stunned at the two of them together, as if she'd never considered the possibility of ever seeing another woman in her father's arms.

Caroline wanted to assure her Wade was just helping her, that there was nothing between them, that she would never take her mother's place, even if she could.

She could say nothing, though, with everyone else looking on.

Still, she was aware of Natalie's hard stare the whole time Wade carried her to the recliner then set her down as carefully as if she were fragile antique glass.

"Is that good?" he asked gruffly and Caroline shifted her gaze from the daughter to the father. His jaw looked tight and she saw his pulse jump there and she wondered if he'd been affected by their nearness as much as she had been.

"Yes. Wonderful—thank you so much. It's amazing how a simple change of scenery can lift my spirits."

"Don't overdo it," Jake warned. "You'll pay the price if you try to take on too much."

"I know, Dr. Dalton. I'll take it easy, I promise."

He rose from the table. "Sorry I can't stick around but I've got to run to the hospital in Idaho Falls to check on one of my patients who had surgery this morning."

"What about my homework?" Natalie asked, a plaintive note in her voice. "I still have, like, ten problems to go."

Wade frowned at her. "I'm still here," he reminded her. "Uncle Jake's not the only one who knows long division, you know."

"Yeah, but he always explains it better," she muttered.

"I'll do my best to muddle through," Wade said dryly.

"Care read?"

Caroline glanced away from the homework drama to find little Cody hovering near the arm of her chair, a favorite picture book in his chubby fingers.

She smiled. "Of course."

"No, not that one," Tanner objected, not far behind. "That one's a baby book. I'll find a better one."

He raced out of the room, most likely to scour his bedroom bookshelves for something more to his liking, leaving Cody standing by her side, his picture book held out like an offering to the gods.

She smiled at him and patted her uninjured leg. "Come on up here, kiddo. Maybe we can get through this one before your brother comes back," she said.

Cody giggled as if they shared a particularly amusing secret and climbed from the footrest onto her lap.

"Is he okay?" Wade asked. The worry in his eyes warmed her even more than Cody's sturdy little body.

"Wonderful." She wedged a throw pillow between her aching ribs and the little boy, then opened the book.

They turned the last page just as Tanner skipped in, his arms loaded with at least a dozen books.

"These are better," he announced, dropping them all to the floor. "Start with this one."

He handed her a rhyming book about trucks she had already read to him at least a dozen times during her time at the Cold Creek, then he pulled an ottoman next to her recliner and perched on it with all the anticipation of a baby bird awaiting nourishment.

The next hour would live in her memory forever as one of those rare, sweet moments when all seems perfect with the world.

A soft rain clicked against the window but a fire in the huge river-rock fireplace took away any chill from the October night and lent a cozy, snug feeling to the gathering room.

While Wade and Natalie slogged their way through the intricacies of arithmetic, Caroline read story after story to the boys, repeating a few of them several times. Tanner wasn't often able to sit still through long bouts of reading but for now he seemed content to settle in next to her, trying to pick out letters he recognized.

A few times she felt the heat of someone watching her and looked up to find Wade studying her intently. As soon as she would meet his gaze, he would quickly turn his attention back to Natalie, but not before she thought she saw an odd, baffled kind of look in his eyes.

Though she knew it wasn't productive and would only lead to more heartbreak when she returned to Santa Cruz, she couldn't prevent her imagination from playing make-believe, if only for a moment. Was this how things would be if they were a family? If she belonged here at the Cold Creek with Wade, with his children?

Autumn evenings spent in front of the fire, winter nights with a soaring Christmas tree there in the corner, springtime with the windows open and the sweet smell of lilac bushes wafting in.

They would sit here, the five of them, sharing stories and memories and laughter.

And then after the children were asleep, Wade would turn to her, those blue eyes bright with need, his strong hands tender on her skin….

She blinked, stunned at herself.

The last little part of her fantasy wasn't so surprising—since that kiss and probably even before then, sexual awareness simmered between them. She couldn't manage to look at him without remembering his mouth, firm and warm on hers, and those large, powerful hands buried in her hair, at the small of her back.

But the rest of it totally took her by surprise. She had no idea such desires lived inside her.

She had made a rewarding career out of helping people discover the true dreams of their heart.

Contrary to what many of her clients thought when they first contacted her, coaching was not about telling people how to live, gleefully doling out advice to anyone who would listen.

She tried to help her clients dig deep into their psyches to discover their potential and break down all the barriers people erected to keep themselves from risking everything to touch those dreams.

How had she so completely missed this deep-seated

need inside herself, then? This intense craving for home and hearth?

She thought she was fulfilled by her life in California but as she listened to the rain and the pop and hiss of the fire and studied the sweet faces of the Dalton children, she realized how much she envied Wade.

He had this all the time, this constant, unwavering love from his children and this unbreakable connection.

She wanted it all—not just the idea of children but the idea of *these* children. Tears burned in her eyes at the warm weight of Cody on her lap and Tanner leaning against her arm. She loved them, all three of them, as much as she loved Wade.

Her heart would rip apart into a thousand jagged pieces when she had to leave the ranch and the Daltons.

She couldn't think about that now. For now, she would sit here and listen to the rain and enjoy the night and these sweet children.

She must have closed her eyes for a moment. The next thing she knew was Wade's voice in her ear, low and disconcertingly close.

"How in the world did you pull that off?" he asked and she blinked her eyes open and found him standing by the recliner.

"Sorry?"

"Must have been a pretty boring story," he murmured.

It took her a moment to realize both boys were asleep—Cody nestled under her chin and Tanner with his cheek resting on her forearm. She probably had dozed off, too. "No wonder nobody complained when I stopped reading."

He smiled, drawing her gaze to his mouth. A deep,

intense yearning to taste him again washed through her and she had to clench her fists to keep from reaching for him.

"Where's Natalie?" Her voice sounded hoarse and a little ragged but she had to hope he didn't notice or would attribute it to lingering sleepiness.

"We finished homework so I sent her off to bed."

"No matter what she said, I thought you explained her homework very well."

His smile was a little lopsided and made her want to trace a finger at the corner of his mouth. "So I guess I could always be a math tutor if the whole ranch thing doesn't work out."

She could just imagine the women of Pine Gulch lining up to have him teach their children.

"What do you think my odds are of getting these guys up to bed without waking them?" he asked.

"I didn't realize you were a betting man."

"Every rancher and farmer I know is a gambler. It's part of the package. You gamble every time you plant a crop or buy an animal or take your stock to market."

"Well, I'll give you a fifty-fifty chance on the boys. I'd have to put my money on Tanner to be the one who wakes up."

"That's what you call a sucker bet." He grinned. "I'd have to be stupid to take it and I try not to be stupid more than once or twice a week. I'll get them settled and then I'll come back and help you back to bed."

"No hurry," she assured him. "I'm still enjoying the change of scenery. Would you mind if I stayed a while?"

"No. Seth is coming in a few minutes to fill me in on

what went on today. We'll probably bore you to tears with all our shop talk."

"I don't mind. I enjoy learning about what goes into running a big ranch like the Cold Creek. Anyway, if I get bored, I have a magazine I can read. As long as you don't mind if I stay."

"No. That's fine."

She smiled and he looked as if he wanted to say something, then decided against it and reached down for Cody. His arm couldn't help but touch her breasts as he scooped the boy off her lap and she was suddenly hot everywhere he touched.

She had almost managed to cool down by the time he returned from carrying Cody upstairs. Her arm was asleep, with the weight of Tanner's head pressing it against the armrest of the recliner, but she hadn't wanted to risk waking him by moving.

Still, she was grateful when Wade returned for him. "One down, one to go," he said softly.

"Good luck."

"I think I'll need it with this one."

Just as he had done with Cody, he lifted Tanner into his arms, and though the boy murmured something and flung an arm across his father's chest, he didn't appear to wake up.

She watched them go, the tall, handsome rancher and his busy little son, quiet only in sleep, and pressed a hand to her heart as if she could already feel it begin to crack apart.

He would miss her when she went back to California.

It was a hard admission but Wade had never let

himself shrink from things that were tough to face. He stood in Tanner's bedroom, which his mother had decorated with everything cowboy, and watched as the boy nestled into his bucking-bronco sheets, rump up in the air like a potato bug.

Focusing on Tanner didn't help him avoid looking the cold, hard truth right in the eye.

Somehow in the few days she'd been on the Cold Creek, Caroline had managed to worm her way into their lives with her softness and her sweet smile and her gentleness with the boys.

The kids adored her, even Nat—though his daughter had seemed a little on the cool side tonight. Cody and Tanner thought she was the best thing to come along since juice boxes. He had watched their eyes light up when he'd carried her into the great room, the eager way both boys had come running just to be near her.

She seemed to adore them, too. Watching her spend the evening reading to his sons had given him a weird tug in his chest. He couldn't explain it and he wasn't sure he liked it, but he couldn't deny that his children had come to love her.

Having her there seemed *right.*

He stared at the rope border Marjorie had nailed around the room. How could that be? Caroline had only been at the Cold Creek a few days but already she seemed to belong, as if she'd been there forever, and he was having a tough time imagining how things would be when she left again.

Alone.

That's how he would be. Not just alone but lonely, and that seemed far, far worse.

He had been empty these last two years since Andi had died. Hollow, joyless, cold. There was a spring on their grazing allotment in the mountains that had suddenly dried up a few years ago when a severe drought had hit the West. But when he had taken the cattle up earlier in the summer, he'd discovered that by some miracle of nature, the wet winter had suddenly revived it and now it was pumping water again just like it had done for generations, clear and pure and sweet.

Since Caroline had come to the ranch, he felt like that spring. He had thought his life was all dried up after Andi had died, that anything good and pure was gone forever.

Now all those empty, dry places inside him seemed to be filling again.

He wasn't sure he was ready to come back to life—nor was he really thrilled about the fact that Caroline was the one who seemed to have brought about the change.

She wasn't at all the sort of woman he needed in his life. She didn't know anything about cattle, she had the same wacky New Age ideas Marjorie did about some things, and she had a busy life and career a thousand miles away.

But she seemed to love his kids, so much that she'd risked her own life to save Tanner's. She was kind and funny and she made his pulse jump every time she smiled at him.

He blew out a breath and tucked the covers closer around Tanner.

He would miss her like crazy.

Chapter Fifteen

When Wade returned to the great room, he found his youngest brother sprawled on the same ottoman Tanner had pulled up next to Caroline's recliner earlier for story time.

Seth appeared so close, Wade was surprised he didn't have his chin perched on Caroline's arm just like Tanner had done.

He couldn't seem to control a quick spurt of jealousy. With his charm and good looks, Seth could have any woman he wanted—and he usually did. If he set his sights for Caroline, she wouldn't stand a chance.

Right now she looked like every other woman who ventured into Seth's orbit—completely charmed. She was laughing at something his brother said and she looked bright and animated and as pretty as a mountain meadow ablaze with wildflowers.

He had to admit, he was slightly gratified when she turned as soon as he entered the room and her crooked little smile actually seemed to kick up a notch or two.

"You can't be done already," she exclaimed. "Did Tanner really stay asleep?"

He shrugged, wondering what Seth would do if he shoved him off the ottoman to the floor and took his place next to her. "So far. I admit, I cheated a little."

"I knew there had to be something underhanded!"

"I didn't put him all the way in his pajamas, just traded his jeans for pajama bottoms and left him in his T-shirt."

"Sneaky," she said in an admiring tone.

"It's one of those survival skills every parent figures out early."

"You were sneaky long before the kids came along," Seth interjected. "You were the one who figured out how to rig that rope in the old maple tree so you could climb out your bedroom window, swing over to the tree and climb down the trunk. It was genius, something I used many a time after I took over your bedroom when you moved out."

"Only I used to sneak out and get in a little late-night fishing while you used it to go make out with SueAnn Crowley. Anyway, I'm sure Caroline isn't interested in this old family history."

"Oh, I am! Did either of you ever get caught?"

Seth grinned. "Nope. That rope is still probably there."

"Guess I'd better take it down before Tanner discovers it and figures out how to use it," Wade said.

He didn't want to go sit on one of the couches and leave Seth here in close proximity to Caroline, so he opted to remain standing by the side of her recliner.

"So are you ready for me to take you to bed?"

At his abrupt question, her lips parted just a little and Seth made a sound that could have been a laugh or a cough.

It took a moment for Wade to realize what he'd said. When he did, he felt the tips of ears go hot and red.

"I meant, can I help you back to your bedroom now?" he said quickly, making a mental note to teach Seth some manners next time the opportunity arose.

"Not yet. Do you mind terribly if I just sit here a while longer? The fire is so comforting and I'm enjoying the change of scenery. I promise, you two can take care of your business and you won't even know I'm here."

Right. And maybe tomorrow his horse would suddenly recite the Pledge of Allegiance. He had no doubt whatsoever that he would be aware of every sigh, every breath, every movement.

"You'll probably be bored to tears listening to dry ranch talk."

"I told you, I find it all interesting. Seth was telling me about the TV interview before you came down. It sounds like it went well."

"He did a good job representing the ranch," Wade said. "And the producer was fine about the change in plan."

How could she be otherwise, with Seth pouring on all his charm? He wouldn't be surprised if his brother had Darci Perez's phone number tucked away right now with all his others.

"I'm still sorry you missed it, especially when you didn't have to on my account," she said.

"She said they got enough footage of me explaining things around the ranch and they'll use that."

"When does it air?" she asked.

"Two weeks from yesterday," Seth provided. "At least that's what Darci said."

"I guess I'll be back in Santa Cruz by then," she said. "I'll have to be sure watch it."

Her casual reminder that she would be out of their lives soon put a definite damper on Wade's mood.

"It's late," he said curtly to Seth. "Let's go through the log so we can all get to bed."

They moved to the table Nat used for homework and Seth pulled out his report of the day's activities.

For the next half hour they discussed feed schedules, which animals to cull for the winter and Seth's encounter with a neighboring rancher disputing water rights.

"Sounds like you handled Simister just right. He needs to know where we stand on this. I wouldn't have done a thing differently."

"Thanks." Seth looked surprised at the comment and Wade wondered if he'd been too stingy with the praise over the years. If so, it was something he'd picked up from old Hank Dalton.

He had worked alongside his father every day until Hank had dropped dead of a heart attack. He could count on one hand the number of times Hank had offered anything to him but criticism.

Had he become like his father in other ways without realizing it? He thought of the extra work Seth had done these last few days with an eagerness that had surprised him, then made him feel guilty, especially when he realized Seth was more than capable of the job.

His brother made sound decisions, treated the ranch

hands with fairness and decency, and had clear ideas about what they were trying to accomplish at the ranch.

Wade should have been delegating to him more, especially these last few years after Andi had died, he suddenly realized. Lord knew, he could have used the help and Seth seemed willing to step in.

Wade wasn't sure why he hadn't seen it, but somehow he had fallen into the habit of thinking of Seth as the same irresponsible kid he'd been when Wade had taken over running the ranch. Maybe because his brother was still a very swinging bachelor, still running around with his friends from high school, still hanging out at the tavern in town.

He acted like he was still in college, though he'd graduated and come back to the ranch five years ago. Seth never seemed to take anything seriously and when Wade compared his brother's life to his own, full of responsibility after responsibility, Seth came out looking reckless and carefree.

Now he wondered how much of his brother's wildness stemmed from Wade's own lack of trust in him.

It was a stunning revelation for him.

Since the day his father had died, Wade had taken his responsibilities to the ranch and his family very seriously. It was tough for him to surrender that burden to someone else because he loathed the idea of anyone thinking he was shirking his duties.

But maybe by failing to delegate more to Seth, he had caused both of them harm.

"You've done a good job these last few days," he said slowly. "I'm sorry for the extra work."

Seth started gathering up the papers he'd brought.

"I'm not. It's been a major learning experience. I've gotten a whole new perspective being the big hombre for a few days."

"You're a good cattleman, Seth. Maybe you ought to give some thought to running your own herd."

Where before Seth had looked astonished at Wade's appreciation, now he looked flabbergasted. His mouth sagged open and he stared for a full moment before he composed himself.

"I've thought about it some," he admitted, then paused. "What would you say if I told you I'm more interested in training horses?"

Wade couldn't say he would be surprised. Seth had been horse-mad since before he could walk. Wade and Jake both enjoyed horses, but Seth had always been passionate about them.

His brother had been a team roper on the college rodeo circuit and had even spent a couple summers on the pro circuit. It seemed like he always had a horse he was working with.

"What kind of operation?"

"Cutters." Seth said the word so fast, Wade realized his brother had indeed given this some thought. "Breeding and training them."

"I thought that was just a hobby with you."

"A hobby I'm damn good at. You know Calliope never met a cow she couldn't work and I trained her from a colt. And remember, I worked that gelding for the Stapeley kid and he got a buckle at the PRCA finals out of the deal."

"What sort of business plan have you considered?"

"Find a good stud, to start with. I've got my eye on one from over at the Diamond Harte in Star Valley. If I could come up with the capital, I think Matt Harte would give me a good deal on it."

"The man has quality horses, that's true."

Seth went on for another ten minutes about what he would do if he ran a breeding-and-training operation, and with every word, Wade felt more and more ashamed.

He had completely undervalued his brother, had been so wrapped up building his own legacy at the Cold Creek that he hadn't seen Seth had dreams of his own.

He wouldn't make that mistake again.

A few weeks ago, he might not have seen the value in a man holding onto his dreams. But things seemed different now. He risked a glance at the recliner where Caroline sat, a magazine propped open on her lap as she gazed into the fire.

You don't think following your dreams is important? she had asked that first day she'd shown up at the ranch.

At the time, he'd thought a man would do better to focus on fulfilling his responsibilities. Now he realized that the work he did at the Cold Creek was both his responsibility *and* his dream. He loved the ranch and had poured his heart into making it a success.

How could he deny Seth the same opportunity?

"You know, you do own a quarter share of the Cold Creek," he said slowly. "Seems to me if you've got your heart set on working with horses, you ought to stop sitting around thinking about it and get serious."

Seth narrowed his gaze. "What are you saying?"

"Off the top of my head, I can think of at least two or three spots on the ranch that would make a good location for stables and an indoor training arena."

His brother had the look of a man afraid to hope. "The Cold Creek has always been about cattle."

"Well, maybe it's time we shake things up a little."

Wade and Seth talked for another half hour about the risks and the challenges of stretching the ranch in a second direction. Seth had thought things through in great detail, and Wade wondered if his brother ever would have acted on those ideas or if he would have been like Wade, so consumed with the daily minutia of running the ranch that he'd lost sight of the bigger picture along the way.

Caroline had helped him refocus, he realized. On his kids, on himself, on more than just the ranch.

The thought distracted him from the business at hand enough that he looked over at the recliner and found her asleep, her cheek resting on one hand.

Seth followed his gaze. "I guess we bored her right to sleep."

"I better take her back to bed."

"And I'll take that as my cue to get out of here. I've got plenty to think about tonight."

If his thoughts involved more than women and whiskey, Wade had to be grateful.

Seth tugged on his denim jacket but paused before putting on his Stetson, his features serious. "At the risk of having you bash my face in, can I offer some advice?"

"You might as well, since I'm pretty sure I'm not going to be able to stop you."

Seth cocked his head toward Caroline. "I don't pretend to know all there is to know about women—"

"And yet you seem to be doing your best to screw up the learning curve for the rest of us."

Seth grinned. "I do what I can."

A second later, his grin slid away as he looked at Caroline again. "Take it from a man who knows women. Caroline is different. She's funny and sweet and smart. She listens when you talk, she's not one of those people who just waits until you wind down before they launch into their own life story. She cares about people, you can tell."

Wade glared, not liking that look in his brother's eyes. "And you're telling me this because…?"

"There's something going on between the two of you. I don't pretend to understand that either, but nobody could miss the vibes the two of you are sending out. She watches you all the time and when she's not watching you, you're watching her. It's a good thing we're into the rainy season because the two of you put out enough sparks to start a forest fire."

Wade flushed, hoping like hell she was really sleeping and not just pretending, and embarrassed that Seth had noticed the attraction he apparently hadn't been able to conceal. "You're crazy."

"Maybe. But I've got to tell you, brother, if a man is lucky enough to find a woman like that, he'd be a damn fool if he didn't hang on to her and never let go."

Before Wade could respond, Seth shoved on his hat and headed out the back door toward his place.

Wade watched him go, a weird ache in his chest as his brother's words rolled around in his head.

Hang on to her and never let go.

Suddenly he wanted desperately to do just that.

How could this have happened?

He slid down to the much-used ottoman next to

Caroline and watched her sleep in the flickering glow of the firelight. How could she have come to be so important?

Looking at her always seemed to take his breath away a little.

She was like something out of a painting hanging in one of the fancy galleries over the mountains in Jackson Hole, all soft, muted colors and elegant lines.

He hated to admit it but Seth was right. Caroline was different.

She had brought laughter and light back to the ranch, had given him hope again in a future that consisted of more than just next year's yield and what interest rates the bank would charge him.

He thought of his talk with Seth and realized suddenly that it was no coincidence they had never had that kind of conversation before. It was more than just Caroline opening his eyes to the importance of having something good to hold onto.

He hadn't talked with Seth about his dreams before because Wade had been so consumed with surviving the present—with the ranch and the kids and all of his many obligations as head of the family—that he hadn't allowed himself to give much thought to the future.

He hadn't wanted to think about the future, not when the present was so bleak.

Now it was as if a door in his mind and heart had opened somehow, showing him a world of possibilities. The only question was whether he was willing to take the chance of walking through that door.

The log in the fireplace finally burned through and broke apart with a loud crackle and a shower of sparks, and the sound seemed to jerk Caroline from sleep.

She blinked her eyes open slowly, like a tiny kitten exposed to light for the first time.

At first she looked confused and he saw the dull wash of pain there before awareness crept in and she sat up a little with just a tiny wince.

"Oh, dear. I've been asleep, haven't I?"

"Yes. I should have taken you back to bed earlier. You need a pain pill, don't you?"

She made a face and looked around the room, ignoring his question. "Did Seth leave?"

"Just barely."

"Before I drifted off, I heard you talking with him about training and breeding horses."

"It's a good idea. Seth has always been a hell of a horseman and if anyone can make it work, he can."

"He was certainly excited about it. More focused than I've seen him since I've been here. It was wonderful to see."

"Well, we've got a lot of planning to do before we bring in the first horse but we'll work up a business plan and see if it's feasible."

"You'll do it even if it's not a huge moneymaker for the ranch, won't you?"

She sounded so confident of it, he flushed that she could read him so accurately. "Probably. It's always good to diversify as long as it's not a big drain on our resources. And I've suddenly realized Seth needs something to call his own. I should have seen it before. Even though he works alongside me on the ranch, his heart has never really been in it. Not like mine is, not like Jake's is with his clinic."

She reached out and touched his arm. "You're a good brother, Wade."

More than he wanted his next breath, he wanted to tug her into his arms and kiss that soft smile. But she was hurting, he reminded himself. He could see it in her eyes. "Come on. Let's get you back to bed so you can take a pill and stretch out."

She must have been hurting more than she let on because she let him scoop his arms under her to lift her carefully from the recliner.

Her arms slid around his neck for balance and she tucked her head under his chin, and it was all he could do not to bury his face in the vanilla-ice-cream scent of her hair.

"I'm sorry you have to do this," she murmured.

I'm not, he almost said, but caught himself just in time. He didn't know how many more chances he would have to be close to her like this.

Hold her close and never let go. Seth's words echoed in his mind. If only things were that easy. Yes, he had feelings for her. But that didn't mean she returned them or that she could ever be happy at the Cold Creek.

He would do well to remember that.

He carried her into her room and set her carefully on the bed. "I'll get you some water so you can take a pill."

"I don't want any more pills."

"I can understand that but you'll sleep better if you do."

"Just tonight, though, then I'm throwing the bottle away."

He poured her water from the pitcher by her bed and handed it to her. "Do you need me to, uh, help you into the bathroom or anything?" he asked after she swallowed the pill.

She shook her head, color rising on her cheeks. "I think I can make it that far on my own. Thank you, though."

He had a million things he wanted to say to her but couldn't think of the right words for any of them.

"Well, good night, then. Call if you need anything."

"I will."

He turned to leave but froze when she reached out and touched her fingers to his arm again. She often touched him to emphasize a point, he was discovering. He didn't care why she did it, he just found he liked it, that he was hungry for any kind of contact with her.

"Wade, I…thank you so much for all you've done for me since I was injured. I know it's been hard for you to turn so much over to Seth but I'm grateful."

"I've learned some things through the experience. My kid brother can handle a whole lot more responsibility than I've been willing to give him over the years. I guess you could say your little run-in with that cow has been good for me and for my brother."

"I'm so pleased I could help you both out," she said dryly.

He laughed out loud and she gazed at him, a strange light in her eyes.

"What?" he asked, intensely aware of her hand still touching his arm.

"I've never seen you laugh before."

He stared at her, thinking back over the week she'd been at the ranch. He hadn't laughed once? It seemed impossible. "Am I really that much of a humorless curmudgeon?"

"You smile at the children sometimes but you don't

laugh. And there's always a sadness in your eyes." She was quiet for a long moment, then she spoke softly. "It breaks my heart."

His heart seemed to tumble in his own chest at her low words. "Ah, Caroline."

For a moment, he was terribly afraid she was going to cry. Her mouth tightened and her eyes glistened but a moment later she smiled, though her eyes were still a little watery.

"Now that I know you have the ability to laugh, I'm going to do everything I can think of to make you do it again."

Her confident statement surprised another laugh out of him and she grinned triumphantly and squeezed his arm. "See? Whatever I'm doing is working already."

"Something is working," he murmured, then he couldn't help himself. He had to kiss her again.

As soon as their mouths tangled, reality rushed in and he froze, stunned at his impulsiveness. He would have jerked back but she slid her arms around his neck with a soft sigh he found incredibly sexy and returned his kiss with fierce intensity, as if she'd been waiting just for this.

Chapter Sixteen

Caroline forgot about the pain digging into her ribs, the throbbing from her leg wound. She forgot about the differences between them and her inevitable heartbreak when she left the ranch.

All she could focus on was Wade touching her, tasting her, like he couldn't seem to get enough.

He murmured her name in that slow, sexy drawl she had come to adore, the one she discovered he only slipped into once in a while when he forgot himself.

She wanted him to forget. She wanted him to think only of her, not the past or the future. Just this moment.

He was bent at an awkward angle, still standing while she was stretched out on the bed, so she slid over to make room for him and tugged him down to the bed beside her.

He pulled her across his lap, supporting her weight

with his arm, and his hands were breathtaking in their gentleness as he traced her chin and tilted her face for his kiss.

His mouth explored her, tasting each hollow, each curve, until she wanted to weep from the emotions pouring through her—love and longing and terrible fear that she would never know this sweet wonder again.

She couldn't speak any of those feelings so she tried to show him with her mouth and her hands what was in her heart.

She couldn't have said how long he held her. A few moments? An hour? Time seemed to have lost all meaning; the only thing that mattered to her was Wade.

Finally, when she was beginning to seriously wish they could share more than these kisses, wonderful though they were, he wrenched his mouth away. "Stop. We have to stop."

"Why?"

His laugh—that sound she adored so much—sounded hoarse, strangled. "You want that list of reasons in alphabetical order or prioritized in order of importance?"

"Neither. I don't want you to stop kissing me." With her arms around his neck, she tried to pull his face down but he was far stronger than she was. He pulled her hands free and held them in his.

"Carrie, we can't. You're just loopy from the pain pill. It's wrong for me to take advantage of you like this."

Okay, maybe she was starting to feel a little buzz. The world suddenly seemed like a beautiful, shiny place, but she didn't know how much of that was from the pain pills and how much came simply from being in Wade's arms again.

"That's ridiculous. I've been dying for you to kiss me again since the last time."

When a muscle flexed in his jaw, she smiled and traced it with her forefinger, loving the rough texture of late-night shadow against her fingertips.

"Since the first night I stayed at the ranch, I've thought about it. Dreamed about it," she whispered.

His breathing caught and she watched his Adam's apple work as he swallowed hard. "You don't know what you're saying right now. You're not yourself."

She certainly couldn't seem to make her brain work the way she wanted it to, but still she smiled softly and reached for his hand. "Here's a confession for you, Wade. I'm more myself when I'm with you than I've ever been in my entire life."

He looked stunned, so shocked she wondered if she should regret being so open with him. No. She meant her words and she wouldn't take them back. Instead, she leaned forward and kissed him. He didn't move for several seconds, then he returned the kiss with tenderness and almost unbearable sweetness.

Finally he pulled away again, resting his forehead on hers. "You make it hard to leave,"

"You don't have to."

"We both know I do. You're hurting and you need to sleep and I …" He paused. "I need to think about all this."

"About what?"

He pulled away, sitting on the edge of the bed, and said nothing for a long time.

When he finally spoke, his blue eyes were solemn. "About the two of us. About where this might be heading and whether that's a journey I'm prepared to take right now."

She nodded, sensing the admission was not a comfortable one for him. She leaned back against her pillows, suddenly exhausted.

"I don't know if this will make any of that thinking easier or harder," she murmured, "but I should tell you that it would be very easy for me to have feelings for you."

"Caroline—"

"I just thought you should know, that's all."

He watched her for a long moment. "And I should tell you that while it would be very easy for me to return those feelings, I'm just not sure whether I'm ready to let myself do that."

She could be content with that, she thought as she closed her eyes and gave in to the exhaustion. It was far more than she'd ever expected.

Caroline woke the next morning with a sweet and giddy anticipation singing through her veins.

For the first few hazy moments after waking, she couldn't quite understand how it was possible to feel so happy when every inch of her body ached, and then recollection flooded back.

She settled back on the pillow and a smile blossomed as she remembered the tenderness of the night before, the intense, smoldering kisses.

Wade cared about her. He couldn't have kissed her, touched her so sweetly if he didn't.

Oh, she knew they still had much to work through

and he could very well decide he wasn't ready for a new love yet. But she would wait. She had waited thirty years to discover what she really wanted out of life. She could wait a while longer for those dreams she hadn't known lived inside her to come true.

How could she ever have imagined when she'd set off on this impulsive journey to try dissuading Quinn from a hasty marriage that she would end up falling in love with a gruff rancher and his three adorable children? With the wild, harsh beauty of the Cold Creek?

She and Wade had a future together. She was sure of it. Now she just had to convince him.

But not without a shower first, she decided. She had contented herself with quick sponge baths since her accident but she needed the full deal today before she could face the day.

Wade had brought in a sturdy plastic lawn chair to give her added support in the bathroom and she maneuvered it into the shower then positioned her injured leg outside the shower curtain so the bandage wouldn't get wet.

It was tricky work and by the time she finished, her ribs ached and her head was pounding, but she was blessedly clean.

When she turned off the spray, she heard a loud banging on the door, so insistent she had to wonder how long it had been going on.

"Caroline?" The voice was low, male and furious. "Caroline, what the hell are you doing?"

She reached for a towel off the rack. "Drying off."

"You've got no business doing that on your own!"

Was he offering to help? she wondered, her stomach

trembling at the thought. Still she was compelled to refuse. "I think I can handle wielding a towel by myself, thanks."

"Not that part," he growled. "I meant the shower. You're going to fall and break your neck."

"I'm done now and I handled things just fine. I'm feeling much better this morning."

It was only a little lie, she told herself. She *did* feel better, but the qualifier was perhaps a bit on the excessive side.

"Why didn't you wait for someone to help you?"

She patted her hair with a towel. "I didn't need help. Everything's under control. I'll be out in a moment."

Suddenly she remembered with chagrin that she'd left her clean clothes on the bed in the adjoining room, thinking it would be much easier to maneuver out there where she had a little more room.

Under normal circumstances, she would wrap in a towel and grab them, but she wasn't entirely sure she could manage to stay covered and work the crutches at the same time.

She finally decided she had no choice but to throw on the robe she'd been wearing. She put it on again and ran a quick comb through her hair, then picked up her crutches.

When she hobbled out, doing her best to stay covered, she found Wade standing outside the door, his arms crossed over his chest. He looked so forbidding she had to wonder if she imagined the heat of the night before, some painkiller-induced fantasy.

No. Her imagination simply wasn't productive enough to conjure up something so magical.

"Where are the kids?"

"Nat's already on the bus and Seth took the boys

into town with him to get some fencing. They always love a trip to the hardware store."

They were alone in the house, she realized, and her insides seemed to shiver as she wondered if he would take this rare opportunity for privacy to kiss her again.

Not with that distant expression back on his features, she feared.

"You do look like you're getting around okay on those," he said, instead of pledging his undying love, as some silly corner of her mind had hoped he had come to do.

"I've been practicing. I'm still not proficient but I'm trying."

"Does it hurt your ribs to use them?"

"A little. But it's worth it to feel mobile again."

Okay, maybe not as mobile as she thought. The shower had sapped her energy more than she'd realized and her knees were trembling a little with the effort to stay upright, so she hobbled to the bed and lowered herself down.

"You don't have to do everything by yourself. Call me next time. That's why I'm here."

"You're sweet to worry about me but I'm fine," she insisted. "A little weak but fine."

"I'm not sweet." He said the words so harshly she blinked. "I don't want you getting the wrong idea because things have maybe been a little different these last few days. The truth is, I'm bad tempered and pig-headed and impatient. I get caught up in a project and I lose track of time. I can be thoughtless and stubborn and I've never been one for much social chitchat."

"That sounds like a disclaimer."

He focused on a spot above her left shoulder. "I just

wanted to make sure you knew these last few days have been outside the norm, that's all. And anything you might have said last night about…about feelings or anything else, I didn't take it seriously."

Ah. Now his words made more sense. "I was never more serious in my life. I haven't taken any pain medicine this morning. My brain is clear and unclouded. And my feelings for you haven't changed."

If anything, she thought, they had deepened with this show of awkwardness. How could a man so big and strong and confident in matters of his ranch be tentative and uncomfortable about this? she wondered.

"Caroline—" he began, his eyes a dark, intense blue. But before he could finish the thought, they heard what sounded like the front door open, then a familiar woman's voice.

"Wade? Caroline? Kids? Anybody home?"

Her gaze locked with Wade as she recognized the voice from her coaching sessions. What horrible timing for Marjorie and Quinn to return.

The honeymoon was over.

A week ago, Wade would have been doing handstands and jumping in circles to hear his mother's voice. But now he wished she would just go away for another week.

In their crazier moments, he and his friends used to cliff dive at a reservoir a few miles away and, talking with Caroline just now, he'd had that same shaky, pulse-pounding feeling he used to experience just before soaring toward the water.

"Caroline—" he said again, not sure what he intended to say.

"Later," she murmured. "Maybe you should go out and say hello while I finish dressing. I'll be out in a moment."

"I'll just go let them know I'm here then come back and help you out, all right?"

She nodded and he walked out in search of his runaway mother.

He found the newlyweds in the great room, looking at the display of family pictures on one wall.

Quinn Montgomery was tall, handsome and athletic looking, with a California tan and a full head of salt-and-pepper hair. He stood with a casual arm around Marjorie and, even from here, Wade could see she looked a decade younger.

She had her hair styled a different way, lighter somehow, and there was a glow about her he was sure he hadn't ever seen before.

Both of them turned when he walked into the room. Marjorie stared. "Wade! I didn't expect to find you home at this hour."

"I do live here," he reminded her dryly.

"I know, but I assumed you would be out working." She looked around. "Where are the boys?"

"Seth went to the ranch supply store in town for some fencing and they decided to ride along."

"Are you sick? Is that why you're home at this hour?"

He didn't want to launch into a complicated explanation about Caroline's injury until she was there so he changed the subject by looking pointedly at her new husband.

Quinn Montgomery had his daughter's eyes, he discovered. They were the same warm brown and right now they were scrutinizing Wade just as intensely, with curiosity and a healthy mix of amusement.

"I believe your son is waiting for an introduction, Marjie."

His mother tittered—she actually *tittered* like some kind of teenager!—and threaded her arm through Montgomery's. "I'm sorry, dear. I don't know where my manners have gone."

She then performed a polite introduction as if they were strangers meeting at a garden party.

Wade had never felt so awkward in his life. Just how was he supposed to respond to the bastard who had eloped with his mother—especially when the bastard in question happened to be the father of the woman Wade...had feelings for?

"Montgomery," he said tersely.

Quinn Montgomery's smile also looked remarkably like his daughter's. "Dalton," he responded in kind. "You have a beautiful ranch here. I'd love to have a tour."

I'll just bet you would, he thought.

"We're very proud of it," he said instead. "The Daltons have been ranching here at the Cold Creek for four generations. We're one of the biggest cattle operations in eastern Idaho."

And we're not about to let some aging, slick-eyed Lothario swindle his way into a share of it, he thought.

"I'm afraid I know next to nothing about cattle ranching, although Marjorie has done her best to give me a primer while we were driving out here. She says you've built the ranch into a real force in the beef industry."

"We're working on it."

"And succeeding, from what your mother says."

Wade scowled. Was Montgomery's interest mere curiosity or something more sinister?

Whatever it was, he didn't want to talk about the Cold Creek's success—or lack thereof—with some total stranger, even if the man was married to one of the ranch's partners.

"So what are your plans, now that the honeymoon is over?" Wade asked pointedly.

His mother giggled. "Oh, it's far from over, believe me," she said with so much gleeful enthusiasm that Wade wanted to cover his ears. He absolutely didn't want to know that much information.

"Marjie, this whole thing is no doubt tough enough on your boys," Montgomery chided gently. "You're not making things any easier."

To his surprise, for a moment, Marjorie looked taken aback, then apologetic. "You're right. I'm sorry, dear," she said to Wade. "As far as our plans, we're going to have to work out the details but I told Quinn I still intend to help you with the children as long as you need me. We were thinking about selling my house in town and building a place of our own out here. That way we're close enough to help you but would still have a little privacy."

If it meant he wouldn't have to have her new husband underfoot all the time, Wade would build the place with his own bare hands.

Montgomery smiled. "There will be time to work out all these details. No need to rush into any decisions today." He paused. "Tell me, is my daughter still here?"

"I'm right here, Dad."

Wade turned to see Caroline standing in the doorway on her crutches.

"Good Lord!" Marjorie exclaimed, her eyes wide and horrified. "What happened?"

"I had a little accident a few days ago, but I'm feeling much better now and Jake says everything is healing nicely."

"Sit down before you fall over on those things," Wade growled. "You were supposed to get dressed and wait for me to come back and get you, not come trekking in here like Sir Edmund Hillary."

"I walked twenty feet, I didn't climb Mount Everest. That may have to wait a while."

She looked wobbly to him, her features pale and her weight leaning a little too heavily on the crutches. He shook his head but hurried forward and scooped her up, then set her carefully in the recliner.

He was rewarded with a blush. "You can stop babying me anytime now, Wade. I'll never learn how to use the crutches if I don't practice. You can't carry me everywhere."

"You think I'm going to let you kill yourself when I'm standing right here to help?"

"You're not always going to be standing right there," she pointed out. "I have to figure it out on my own sometime."

She changed the subject by looking past Wade to Montgomery. "Hello, Dad." There was a reserve in her eyes Wade wasn't expecting, though he thought he saw love there, too.

Quinn stepped forward and kissed her cheek. "Hello, baby. I was surprised to learn you were here at the ranch."

"Were you?" The coolness in her voice again surprised Wade. Since she'd come to the ranch, she'd been nothing but warm and friendly to everyone, from the ranch hands to Natalie's bus driver.

"There was no reason for you to come chasing after me. I thought I explained everything sufficiently in my e-mail. You shouldn't have been so concerned."

"When you decided to run off with one of my clients without a word to me beforehand, you really didn't have the slightest inkling that I might consider that a cause for anxiety?"

"Carrie—"

"No, tell me Dad. Why didn't you mention to me that the two of you were corresponding?"

"We knew you would be upset," Marjorie broke in. "Quinn knew he had done the wrong thing answering your work phone that day you weren't home but we had such a lovely conversation, neither of us wanted to see it end. There was nothing underhanded about it, it was just too precious to share with anyone at first, especially when we knew you wouldn't be happy about how we met."

Caroline said nothing to that, only gave her father a long look. There were undercurrents zinging between her and her father that Wade couldn't pretend to understand. He did know she looked upset, though, and for that alone he decided to step in.

Before he could, Marjorie did the job for him. "I'm starving," she said suddenly. "We've been driving all night and didn't take time for breakfast. Would anybody else like an omelet?"

Caroline shook her head but her father smiled. "An omelet sounds great. Can I help you make it?"

"No, no. Why don't you stay here and talk to your

daughter? I'm sure the two of you have a great deal to say to each other. Wade, why don't you help me in the kitchen and fill me in on everything that's happened around here since I've been gone?"

That particular conversation would take far longer than the time needed to whip up a couple of omelets, but he followed Marjorie anyway, impatient to talk to his mother.

"Isn't he wonderful?" Marjorie asked as soon as they were out of earshot. "He's kind and thoughtful and by some miracle, he's as crazy about me as I am about him."

Wade shook his head. "What the hell were you thinking, to run off with a man you only knew from the Internet, a man none of us had ever met? For all you knew, he could have been an ax murderer. Or worse!"

Marjorie grabbed a carton of eggs from the refrigerator. "I'm not some desperate old lady who just fell off the turnip truck, Wade. You don't think I considered that possibility?"

"But you married the bastard anyway!"

She narrowed her gaze at him. "Be careful, son. That bastard is my husband." The steel in her voice might have been coated in velvet but it was still most definitely steel.

He sighed. "Let me rephrase, then. You considered the possibility that the man you were sharing a clandestine long-distance relationship with might have a criminal past but you went ahead and married him anyway. Explain how an intelligent, progressive woman like you claim to be can make that choice."

"Because I love him," she said simply. "Quinn is a good man, honey. I knew that right away. Yes, he's had some run-ins with the law but he's paid his debt to society and moved on."

He stared at her, his blood suddenly running cold. "What do you mean, run-ins with the law?" he asked carefully.

She made a careless, dismissive gesture, an egg in her hand. "Just that. He was a little wild in his past but that's all behind him now. And before you think I was some naive old bat who let myself be charmed by a handsome face and a smooth talker, Quinn himself told me of his past the very first time we talked on the phone. He didn't have to—we were only casual acquaintances at the time—but he did."

Wade couldn't seem to think straight with the rushing in his ears and he was suddenly filled with a bone-deep foreboding. "Mother. Exactly what did he do?"

"Oh, this and that." She whipped the egg beater. "Ran a few schemes that went bad, a little grifting here and there. He was a bit of a rascal in the past and the law finally caught up with him. But I'll have you know, he's turned over a new leaf and has been a clean, productive member of society since he was released from prison four years ago."

Prison? *Prison?* Just when he thought this situation couldn't get worse. Now he had the delightful added complication of learning his mother was married to an ex-con.

He let out a long, slow breath, so angry he didn't trust himself to speak. A criminal. His new stepfather was a criminal.

Why was he just learning about this now? Caroline had been in his home for more than a week and not once had she whispered a single word about her father's dubious past.

He had a right to know, damn it. She should have told him. He had trusted her, had told her things no one else in the world knew. With all they shared, how could she have kept this part of her life a secret?

The deep ache of betrayal settled in his gut and he wasn't sure which was more powerful, that or the fury seething through him.

His instincts had been dead on. A grifter. A scam artist. In Marjorie, the bastard had found a nice, juicy widow, then he'd wooed and wed her before her family could do a thing about it.

Caroline must have been in on the whole scheme. Otherwise, wouldn't she have told him about her father's past?

His stomach hurt suddenly like he'd been sucker punched, and he had to fight to press a hand there to help him catch his breath.

"Quinn deeply regrets the wrongs he did and has worked hard to make restitution," Marjorie went on, heedless of his turmoil. "Personally, I believe it shows a great strength of character to admit to his wrongs and try to repair the harm he caused. If you give him a chance, I know you'll love him."

She smiled as she added the eggs to the frying pan. "I'm sure you and the kids already love Caroline, don't you? She's such a sweetheart and she's so much like her father."

Yeah. He was finally beginning to figure that out.

Chapter Seventeen

By the time he returned to the great room, Wade was fairly confident he had the worst of his rage and hurt contained behind a vast wall of ice.

Even though he wanted to pick up his new stepfather and throw him through the big picture window, he forced himself to be polite.

He was also polite to his mother, even though his second impulse was to lock her in her room until she rediscovered her brain.

Caroline, he mostly ignored, even though what he most wanted was to grab her and shake her and ask her why the hell she had to go and make him feel again, just so he could bleed.

Finally, just when he thought he might explode if he had to pretend another second, Marjorie finished her omelet and smiled at her new husband. "Why don't we go bring in our luggage and then have a look around the ranch?"

Quinn agreed with alacrity, just as Wade would have expected. Eager to get an eyeful of his score, Wade thought bitterly, grateful he'd had the foresight to contact the ranch attorneys right after Marjorie's fly-by-night wedding to make sure the Cold Creek assets were protected.

Caroline and her scheming father wouldn't see a penny.

"They seem genuinely happy, don't you think?" Caroline said as soon as they left. Her tone conveyed a relief and surprise he didn't quite understand and couldn't take time to analyze.

When he didn't answer, she gave him a searching look and then her smile froze.

"You don't agree that they seem happy?"

"Oh, they seem delirious," he snapped. "It's a regular lovefest here at the Cold Creek."

Her smile slid away completely. "What's wrong?"

His fury finally managed to burn a hole in the ice covering his emotions and he couldn't stop it from seeping through, even if he wanted to.

"Were you ever going to tell me?"

At his low, bitter tone, her face paled. "Tell you… what?"

"About my new stepfather and his interesting little hobbies. Oh, and, I don't know, perhaps you might have thought to mention the time he spent behind bars."

She drew in a sharp breath and her features lost even more of their color. "Wade—"

"What? Did it slip your mind? After all, he's such a fine, upstanding citizen now."

She folded her hands in front of her and, through his howling pain, he saw they were trembling slightly.

"What do you want me to say?" she asked in a small voice.

"What's your game, Caroline? Your father is easy to read. He finds a wealthy but vulnerable widow and charms his way into her life. It's an old and familiar story but I'm afraid this time it's not going to work. My mother can't cash in her share of the ranch unless the other three shareholders agree and I can guaren-damn-tee that neither I nor my brothers will ever do that. No matter how clever he might be, your swindler of a father won't see a penny of Cold Creek money."

Her dark eyes seemed huge, bruised, in her pale face and he had a twinge of anxiety but quickly discarded it.

"Your father's role is easy to figure out. But what is your part in this little drama? What were you hoping to gain by all this? By coming here and insinuating yourself into my life, into my children's lives?"

"Nothing," she whispered.

"Oh, come on." He bit out the words and had the hollow satisfaction of seeing her flinch. "If you were purely innocent, why didn't you ever mention your father's past crimes? You hoped I would never find out, didn't you? Because you know that once I learned the truth, your little game would be over."

He wanted her to defend herself, to tell him he was crazy, to explain, but she said nothing, her mouth compressed in a tight line.

He let out a harsh breath. "If your father's half as good at the grift as you, no wonder my mother fell for him. You'll be happy to know, whatever game you were running, it worked. I fell for all of it, the whole sweet, nurturing act."

He couldn't remember ever being so angry—most of all at himself. He should have listened to his own instincts at first, his suspicions of her. If he had held on to them and protected himself a little better, he wouldn't be feeling this terrible, crushing sense that he had lost something rare and precious.

"I trusted you, Caroline. I let my children come to care for you, let *myself* care about you. For the first time in two years, the world seemed bright and shining and new. I thought you were someone good and decent, a woman I could love."

His last word came out savage and ugly and she made a small, wounded sound.

She was crying, he saw, and the sight of it arrowed right through his fury to his heart. Damn her. He couldn't let her get to him. He wouldn't fall for it, even though part of him wanted to hold her tight, to tell her he was sorry, to kiss her tears away.

She was only crying out of frustration because her plans had been ruined, he told himself.

"The tears are a nice touch," he snarled. "Too bad I've got your number now. You can shut them off anytime."

"Oh, can I?" she whispered, blinking hard.

Tears shimmered on her lashes and one more slid down the straight plane of her nose. She swiped at with a jerky, abrupt motion, but another one quickly took its place.

Suddenly his anger washed away, leaving only a deep, yawning sense of loss and he couldn't look at her anymore, with her soft eyes and her pretty features and her lying mouth.

"The minute Jake says you can travel again, I want you off my ranch," he said quietly.

"Of course," she murmured.

He turned away, thinking of how baffled and lost his children would be when she disappeared from their lives. Though he hated to ask her for anything, he knew he had no choice, for their sakes.

"I would appreciate it if you'd stay away from Nat and the boys during the rest of your time here. They're going to be hurt enough when you leave. I don't want them to suffer more for my stupidity."

He didn't trust himself to say anything more, just turned and walked out without looking back.

She certainly wasn't going to wait for permission from any of the Dalton brothers.

As soon as the door slammed behind Wade, Caroline allowed herself only a few ragged breaths for strength, then grabbed her crutches and pulled herself to her feet, welcoming the physical pain if it would take some of this terrible ache from her chest.

By sheer force of will, she made it to her bedroom and by the time Quinn wandered in a half hour later in search of her, she was sweating and pale but her suitcases were packed and waiting on the bed.

Quinn stopped in the doorway, his gaze taking in her luggage. "What's this about?" her father asked.

Though it cost just about everything she had left, she managed to speak in a calm, even tone. "I need a ride to the airport in Idaho Falls. I'm not physically able to drive yet."

Quinn looked surprised. "Do you really think that's

wise? Hate to break it to you, baby, but you're not looking so hot right now. Maybe you ought to sit down and rest. Think this through a little."

"No. I need to leave."

Something in her tone or her expression must have given away her distress. Quinn's too-handsome features dissolved into concern and he stepped closer.

"What's the matter? Come here. You look like you just lost your best shill."

He wrapped her in his arms and for an instant she leaned her weight against him, surrounded by the familiar scent of his aftershave and the cinnamon mints he was never without.

The combination of smells made her feel ten years old again, and she wondered how she could love her father so much and still carry this heavy burden of anger.

She stepped away, balancing on her crutches. "Quinn, I haven't asked you for anything. Not anything, not even that time I spent four months in jail for something we both knew I had nothing to do with. I'm asking you now, calling in every marker. I need a ride to the airport. I can't stay here another minute."

To her chagrin, her voice broke on the last word and tears burned in her eyes again.

Quinn studied her for a long moment. "Oh, baby. I've never been much of a father to you, have I? There are plenty of sins Saint Peter can pile at my feet when I reach those pearly gates, but the worst will be the harm I've done to my little girl."

He slid his thumb over her cheek. "I was given a rare and precious gift, better than any score I could dream up, and I treated it like pigeon bait."

She couldn't deal with this. Not now.

"I need to go home. Please, Daddy."

Her tears were falling freely now and Quinn pulled her into his arms again. When he released her, he looked sad and tired and years older.

"Let me go find my keys."

Caroline wasn't sure how she survived the two weeks after she left the Cold Creek. She had little memory of the torturous plane ride home or of that first terrible night when she had wept until she'd thought for sure she must have no tears left. The intervening days all seemed to run together, a hazy blur of sorrow and loss.

Physically, she felt much better. Though her doctor in Santa Cruz still advised her not to put weight on her leg, she was moving around on her crutches with ease and the pain had abated significantly.

Her chest still ached but she wasn't sure if that was from her broken ribs or her broken heart.

She sighed now, gazing out the window at the little slice of ocean that was all she could see from her cottage.

A cold rain blew against the glass, as it had been doing nearly every day since she'd returned from the Cold Creek. She was so tired of it. If the sky would only clear, maybe she could feel warm again. She might even remember that the sun always came out again, even after the darkest night.

There was no sunshine in sight today. From here, the sea looked a churning, angry green, and the sky was heavy and dark.

In hopes of cheering herself up, she had opened a jar of the tomato soup she'd canned with produce from her own garden. It was warming on the stove, sending out a hearty, comforting smell, and a fire burned merrily in her little fireplace, but she still felt cold, empty.

Somehow, she had to learn to go on, but the thought of a future without Wade and the children seemed unendurable.

She missed the children so much she could hardly bear it. Nat, with her rapid-fire conversation and her bossiness, Tanner and all that mischievous energy, Cody the cuddler, who was never as happy as when he was sitting on a warm lap with a book and his blanket.

And Wade.

Her finger traced a raindrop's twisting journey on the other side of the glass. She missed Wade most of all. She missed his strength and his slow smile and the sweet tenderness of his touch.

She had to snap out of this misery. Her work was suffering—it was very difficult to help others face their problems and weaknesses when her own life was such a shambles.

She'd had two sessions that morning and had to reschedule both, with great apologies to her clients, because she just hadn't been able to focus.

Tonight would be better, she told herself. She would have her soup, turn on some cheerful music, then try to finish some of the paperwork she had been neglecting since her return to California.

She had just dished up a bowl and set it on the table to cool when her office telephone rang. She waited for the answering machine to pick up but the ringing continued.

Rats. In the distracted state she seemed to permanently inhabit since leaving the Cold Creek, she must have forgotten to switch it back on after sending a fax earlier.

With an exasperated sigh, she grabbed her crutches to hobble in and turn it off. The ringing stopped just as she made her slow way to her office door, but it started up again before she could reach the phone. Whoever it was had persistence going for him.

She could turn on her machine and let technology catch the call or she could pick it up.

Maybe human contact would shake her out of her melancholy, make her feel a little less alone. She lowered herself to her office chair and picked up the phone.

"Light the Stars."

A long pause met her words and she heard a burst of static, then a male voice spoke, sounding like it was coming from some distant planet.

"Yes. Hello. I'm interested in your coaching services."

She almost told him to call back in the morning during business hours. But even through the dicey connection, she thought she heard a hint of desperation in the voice.

"Have you ever used a life coach before?" she asked, trying to gauge a little background on the potential client.

"No. But I need some serious help and you come highly recommended. I understand you're the best."

Not anymore, even if that were ever true. Right now she was a mess and she wasn't sure she could coach a mosquito to bite.

"There are many good life coaches out there. Finding the right one is always a little tricky. I always recommend that my clients talk to several before finding the one they want to work with."

"I don't want to do that. It's you or nobody else. I'm desperate here, ma'am."

She didn't need that kind of pressure—not now, when she was filled with self-doubt. But something about that staticky voice struck a chord within her.

"All right. We can set up a time for a trial session if you'd like—"

"Can't we do that now?"

She laughed a little, though it sounded hollow and tinny to her ears, and she wondered how long it had been since she'd found anything genuinely amusing.

"I'm afraid it doesn't work that way. After we schedule an initial session, I usually have my clients fill out a somewhat lengthy questionnaire on my Web site and e-mail it to me so I have a little background information going into our session."

"What kind of questions?"

"Basic things, really. Name, occupation, your family dynamics. The areas of your life you're unhappy with...."

"I can tell you that one right off. My life is a mess, mostly because I've been an idiot."

Oh, I bet I've got you beat on that one, she thought.

"I've been stupid and mean to someone who didn't deserve it and in the process I threw away something that could have been wonderful. I'm miserable. The woman I love left me and I need your help trying to figure out if there's any chance I could win her back."

Caroline closed her eyes. Why couldn't his problem be something simple like a midlife crisis or dissatisfaction with his career choices? Why did it have to be a romance turned sour?

She couldn't deal with this right now, not with the shambles her own life was in.

"I don't think I can help you," she said quietly.

"You have to. Look, I'm desperate. This woman brought joy and laughter back to a cold and lonely world. She made me feel again, when I wasn't sure I ever would again. I can't face a future without her in it. I can't."

Even through the bad connection, the raw emotion in his voice came through clearly and Caroline was shocked to feel tears burn behind her eyelids. She definitely couldn't take on this client—or any client dealing with a relationship disappointment right now.

"I'm sorry," she said after a moment, "but I'm afraid you're going to have to find someone else to work with you. I can give you some referrals to some excellent coaches—"

"No. I don't want anybody else. I want you."

"I don't think I'm the right person to help you at this time."

The man gave a ragged-sounding laugh. "I'm afraid you're the only one who can help me."

"I don't—" she began but the doorbell rang before she could complete the sentence, then rang again more insistently just an instant later.

"You should probably get that," the voice on the phone said.

"Yes. I'm sorry. Could you hold on a moment?"

"As long as it takes," he responded.

Cordless phone in the crook of her shoulder, she hobbled the few steps to the door and looked out the peephole, then nearly lost her balance on her crutches.

"Wade," she breathed.

He stood on her stoop, his Stetson dripping rain, looking big and gorgeous and wonderful.

And holding a cell phone to his ear.

"Caroline," the voice on the phone murmured and she wondered how she had possibly mistaken that slow drawl for a stranger's voice.

Her heart stuttered in her chest and she could do nothing but stare at his distorted image through the peephole. He was here, not a thousand miles away on his Idaho ranch, but right here on her doorstep.

After two weeks of misery, of missing him so badly she couldn't breathe around it, he stood in front of her. She almost couldn't believe it.

"Are you still there?" he asked after a long moment.

"I...yes. I'm here."

"I'm sorry, Caroline," he said softly in her ear and she saw the truth in his eyes. "I'm so sorry. I should have trusted you. I should have trusted myself, my own instincts. In my heart, I knew you were just what you seemed but I jumped at the chance to push you away. It's a poor excuse, but I can only tell you I was scared."

"Scared?"

"When I lost Andrea, I didn't think I would survive the pain of it and I sure never dreamed I might be able to love again. And then you showed up at the Cold Creek. Somehow you started to thaw all those frozen corners of my heart and it scared the hell out of me."

"Wade—"

"It still scares me," he admitted. "But the thought of living without you scares me more."

She pressed a hand to her stomach, to the swirly, jittering emotions jumping there.

"I love you, Caroline," he said quietly. "With all my heart. Are you going to open the door? Or will you leave me standing out in the rain for the rest of my life?"

With pounding heart and trembling hands, she worked the locks as fast as she could, dropping the phone in the process. Finally, after what felt like forever, the last bolt shot free and she jerked open the door.

It wasn't a mirage, some heartache-induced dream. He was real. And he was hers.

Using her crutches as a fulcrum, she launched herself at him, laughing and crying at the same time. He caught her, as she knew he would, and pulled her tight against him.

"Carrie," he murmured, his blue eyes bright and intense in the gloom, then his mouth found hers.

It was a kiss of redemption, of healing. Of peace and hope and joy, and she never wanted to stop.

"I love you," she said against his mouth. "I've missed you so much."

He made a low sound in his throat and kissed her fiercely, until she was dizzy from it.

"We're getting soaked," he murmured some time later.

"I don't care."

His laugh was raw. "You'll catch pneumonia, then your father will never forgive me. He's already spent two weeks telling me what an idiot I am."

She blinked. "Quinn?"

"My new stepfather is not too thrilled with me right now. Nobody on the ranch is, if you want the truth. For the last two weeks, I've been getting the cold shoulder from just about everybody. Even Cody."

She couldn't believe that. The little boy adored his father.

"The kids aren't speaking to me, my brothers only talk to me to tell me what a damn fool I am, and your father finally threatened bodily violence if I didn't get a brain in my head and come after you."

"He…he did?"

Without waiting for an invitation, Wade carried her through the door to her couch, then sat down with her in his lap. They would drip all over it, but she didn't care.

"That man might have made some mistakes where you're concerned but he loves you. He told me everything, all his years of running cons, how you used to beg him to stop but he was always after the thrill of the next deal. He told me you were the most honest person he'd ever met and would rather cut out your tongue than join him in a con."

"You believe him?"

He cupped her chin. "He told me about Washington."

She closed her eyes, mortified that he knew about her time in jail, but they opened again when he kissed her lightly.

"He told me none of it was your fault, that he dragged you into the whole mess against your will."

"I couldn't testify against him. I would have been out in a day but I couldn't do it. I'm weak when it comes to him."

"Not weak. You love him. And so does Marjorie, by the way. He seems to be crazy about her, too. After two endless weeks of living with their constant billing and cooing, I have to believe it's the real deal. Nobody could be that good an actor, even your father."

"Do you mind? About his past?"

He was quiet for a moment, his hand doing delicious

things to the small of her back. "He makes her happy. She didn't have much of that, married to my father, so I can't begrudge her this."

He made a face. "And to tell you the truth, though I hate to admit it, your dad is growing on me."

"Yes, he seems to have that effect on people," she said dryly.

"I know I hurt you and I'm sorry, sweetheart," he said after a moment. "If you can find it in your heart to forgive me, I swear I'll spend the rest of my life trying to make it up to you."

"Oh, Wade. There's nothing to forgive. Nothing! I should have told you about Quinn the moment I arrived at the ranch. That's the whole reason I came after him, I was in a panic that he might be running another con game, with Marjorie as his mark."

"He signed a prenuptial agreement. Apparently he insisted on it. Marjorie showed it to me and Quinn willingly gave up any current or future claim to any ranch assets or income."

Caroline sagged against him, as the last of the worry over Quinn's motives—the worry she hadn't even realized had been lurking inside her—seemed to seep away, leaving a vast relief.

"I guess it takes a man in love to recognize another one, and I think what Quinn and Marjorie have is the real deal."

"Oh, that's wonderful."

He smiled, then kissed her softly. "I love you. On behalf of everybody on the Cold Creek—but especially for the sake of this lonely, miserable shell of a man—I'm asking you to come back. The kids miss you. I miss you and I need you more than life, Caroline. You showed me how to dream again and I don't want to give that up. Will you come back to the Cold Creek and to me?"

She touched his face, this gorgeous strong man who was looking at her with such tenderness, then she smiled and pressed her mouth to his. "There's nowhere on earth I'd rather be."

* * * * *

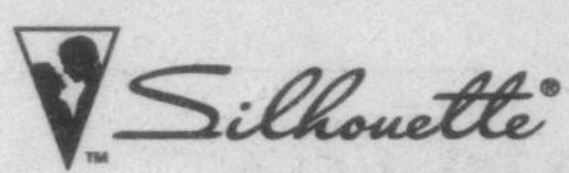

SPECIAL EDITION®

COMING NEXT MONTH

#1753 CUSTODY FOR TWO—Karen Rose Smith
Baby Bonds
It was a double blow to wildlife photographer Dylan Malloy—the sister he'd raised died suddenly *and* didn't leave her newborn in his care. Though her friend Shaye Bartholomew gave the child a good home, Dylan wanted to help. He proposed marriage—but was it just to share custody, or had Shaye too found a place in his heart?

#1754 A WEDDING IN WILLOW VALLEY—Joan Elliott Pickart
Willow Valley Women
It had been ten years since Laurel Windsong left behind Willow Valley and marriage plans with Sheriff Ben Skeeter to become a psychologist. But when her career hit the skids, she came home. Caring for an ailing Navajo Code Talker, she began to work through her personal demons—and rediscovered an angel in the form of Sheriff Ben.

#1755 TWICE HER HUSBAND—Mary J. Forbes
When widow Ginny Franklin returned to Misty River to open a day-care center, she didn't expect to run into her first husband, Luke Tucker—literally. The car crash with her ex landed her in the hospital, but Luke considerately offered to take care of her children. Would renewed currents of love wash away the troubles of their shared past?

#1756 HER BEST-KEPT SECRET—Brenda Harlen
Family Business
Journalist Jenny Anderson had a great job in Tokyo and a loving adopted family, but she'd never overcome trust issues related to her birth mother. For Jenny, it was a big step to get close to Hanson Media attorney Richard Warren. But would their fledgling affair run afoul of his boss Helen Hanson's best-kept secret...one to which Jenny held the key?

#1757 DANCING IN THE MOONLIGHT—RaeAnne Thayne
The Cowboys of Cold Creek
Family physician Jake Dalton's life was thrown into tumult by the return of childhood crush Magdalena Cruz, a U.S. Army Reserves nurse badly injured in Afghanistan. Would Jake's offer to help Maggie on her family ranch in exchange for her interpreter services at his clinic provide him with a perfect pretext to work his healing magic on her spirit?

#1758 WHAT SHOULD HAVE BEEN—Helen R. Myers
Widow Devan Anderson was struggling to raise a daughter and run a business, when her first love, Delta Force's Mead Regan II, suffered a grave injury that erased his memory. Seeing Devan brought everything back to Mead, and soon they were staking a new claim on life together. But if Mead's mother had a say, this would be a short-lived reunion.